Elen Caldecott graduated with an MA in Writing for Young People from Bath Spa University. Before becoming a writer, she was an archaeologist, a nurse, a theatre usher and a museum security guard. It was while working at the museum that Elen realised there is a way to steal anything if you think about it hard enough. Elen either had to become a master thief, or create some characters to do it for her – and so her debut novel, *How Kirsty Jenkins Stole the Elephant*, was born. It was shortlisted for the Waterstones Children's Prize and was followed by *The Mystery of Wickworth Manor*, *The Great Ice-Cream Heist* and most recently *The Marsh Road Mysteries*. Elen lives in Bristol with her husband, Simon, and their dog.

www.elencaldecott.com

Check out the **Elen Caldecott Children's Author** page on Facebook

Also by Elen Caldecott

The Marsh Road Mysteries
Diamonds and Daggers
Crowns and Codebreakers
Spooks and Scooters

* * *

How Kirsty Jenkins Stole the Elephant
How Ali Ferguson Saved Houdini
Operation Eiffel Tower
The Mystery of Wickworth Manor
The Great Ice-Cream Heist

CATS and CURSES

THE MARSH ROAD MYSTERIES

CATS and CURSES

ELEN CALDECOTT

BLOOMSBURY

LONDON OXFORD NEW YORK NEW DELHI SYDNEY

Bloomsbury Publishing, London, Oxford, New York, New Delhi and Sydney

First published in Great Britain in August 2016 by Bloomsbury Publishing Plc
50 Bedford Square, London WC1B 3DP

www.bloomsbury.com
www.elencaldecott.com

BLOOMSBURY is a registered trademark of Bloomsbury Publishing Plc

Text copyright © Elen Caldecott 2016
Illustrations copyright © Nathan Reed 2015

The moral rights of the author and illustrator have been asserted

A CIP catalogue record for this book is available from the British Library

ISBN 978 1 4088 7604 6

Typeset by RefineCatch Limited, Bungay, Suffolk
Printed and bound in Great Britain by CPI Group (UK) Ltd, Croydon CR0 4YY

1 3 5 7 9 10 8 6 4 2

To Anna and Tom

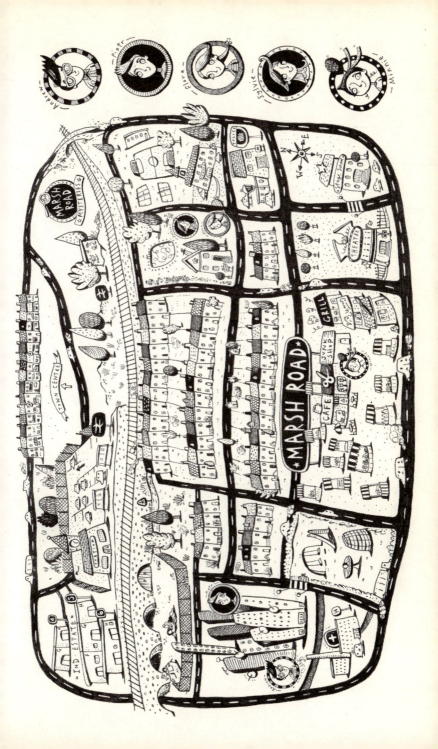

Chapter One

Andrew Jones had positioned his mum, carefully, at the centre of a magic carpet. Using just the power of his mind, he was making sure that Mum floated across the car park without a jolt, or a knock, or even a wobble. It was imperative that this precious cargo was delivered safely.

'You all right, Mum?' he asked.

'I'm holding on tight. Everything is shipshape so far,' Mum replied. She tightened her grip on his shoulder and leaned into him. He took the weight of her with a straight back.

'Imagine that the carpet is whisking you all the way there. All you have to do is stay on,' Andrew advised.

Mum nodded. 'I can practically see the gold and red silk. Is it gold and red?'

'Of course.'

'Then I can practically see it. Do you mind if we just stop for a second?'

He looked around, conjuring a bench at exactly the right point in the road – though he was willing to admit it might have been the council who put it there – and headed towards it. Mum settled on to it with a sigh. She propped her stick against the wood.

'It's not far now,' Andrew said.

'I know. I just need a second to catch my breath.'

They were beyond the car park. The bench was at the edge of the road, and behind them rose a small embankment. The grass was patchy, with dark muddy spots between tufts, but Andrew was sure that he could smell the daffodils deep beneath the earth. Spring was on its way and Mum was getting better.

He looked at her pearl-pale knuckles, placed in her lap.

'We could wait a bit longer?' he said. 'Tilda wouldn't mind.'

'I'd mind,' Mum said, in a tone of voice that Andrew recognised from a hundred telling-offs. 'I've been cooped up in that flat for long enough. It's time.' She wedged the end of her stick against the pavement and levered herself upright. 'Come on, where's this magic carpet then?'

Andrew slotted himself against her, carrying her along.

They headed down Marsh Road, towards Meeke and Sons Curios and Gimcracks – otherwise known as Tilda's junk shop. It had been a year since Mum had given up work, a year since her accident and since Andrew began looking after her at home. But today she was going to work, volunteering with Tilda. Like lowering herself into a swimming pool, rather than diving in off the top boards, it was meant to ease her in gently. Doing it during half-term, so he could help her get there. He glanced up at her. She was looking confident. Or determined, which was the same sort of thing.

They moved together through Marsh Road Market. It was a cold day, with weak orange-squash sunlight straining to be felt above the roofs of the buildings. At the end of the street, an old block had been demolished and the low sun poured over the construction site more warmly.

Mum was smiling now, a proper orange-segment smile, at the traders she knew, and the people she didn't. Andrew felt like there was marshmallow where his chest should be. Mum was really doing it. She was getting back to normal.

He tightened his grip on her waist, just to let her know he was still there.

They stopped, together, outside the junk shop. Meeke and Sons Curios and Gimcracks was shuttered up still; the white rollers were down and the door was locked up behind a grille.

Minnie stuck her head out of the salon next door. 'Mrs Jones!' she squealed. 'You look amazing! How are you?'

Andrew puffed out his chest. Mum did look amazing.

'Hi, Minnie,' Mum said softly. 'It's lovely to see you too. Outside, that is!'

Minnie was part of Andrew's gang. Well, it was more Piotr's gang, really, Piotr was their leader. But Andrew was his second in command. After Flora. He was joint second in command with Flora and Minnie. But he was definitely more in command than Flora's twin sister, Sylvie. They were all friends, but they were also top crime solvers too. Marsh Road would be a dangerous place without them.

He eyed the market the way a sheriff eyes a saloon. If anyone messed with Mum, they'd have the whole gang to answer to.

'Sarah! You're here!'

4

Andrew whipped round. He hadn't noticed the door to the junk shop opening. His flank had been exposed, like on an embarrassing baby photo. Tilda, the junk shop owner, smiled from the doorway. The tiny mirrors on her dress sparkled and her amber beads looked like frozen honey. A green-and-blue silk shawl completed the look.

Mum leaned in and whispered to him, 'Am I underdressed?'

'No way!' Her stripy top and freshly ironed jeans were perfect. She was perfect. He gave her hand a small squeeze. She smiled. It was his job to make her smile.

'Come in, come in.' Tilda waved.

They stepped inside, Minnie following too.

'I'll get the kettle on!' Tilda said. 'Always best to start the day as you mean to go on – with lots of tea! Then I can show you around the shop and how to work the till and that sort of thing. It's all quite simple.' She headed away from the counter.

The shop, stuffed full of objects and furniture and random old things, looked anything but simple. Brown sideboards and cupboards and dressers were piled like expensive Jenga blocks, forming narrow corridors. The sight lines were terrible; it felt like a first-person shooter,

5

though with occasional tables instead of zombies. Andrew felt his trigger finger twitching. He had to try not to maim any merchandise today. In every spare nook and cranny were old crockery and crystal glasses, pictures in frames, dolls and dining sets, dartboards and drums, dogs made of china and china decorated with dogs. And more than a little dust over everything. From the ceiling hung swags of fabric – Victorian wedding dresses, Sixties minidresses, flared trousers and paisley waistcoats. The smell of camphor and mothballs wrestled with beeswax.

'I think I could start with a good spring clean,' Mum whispered. 'You don't need to wait with me,' she added. 'Go and play with Minnie.'

Go and play? He rolled his eyes at her. He'd been helping her with washing, and cooking tea, and buying groceries and all kinds of things for a year! And she was telling him to go and play?

She laughed. 'I mean it, Andrew. You've been amazing. But you don't have to worry any more.'

Really?

But that was his job too.

She nodded and waved at him, shooing him out.

He felt a fizz in his chest. He felt his arms relax. Maybe she was right. Maybe he could leave her here and she was going to be absolutely fine. Wow. Could he belt out a song in the middle of Mum's first day at work? He took in a deep breath, and prepared to sing …

When the bell above the door tinkled.

Someone came in.

'I'll be right there!' Tilda called from the back of the shop.

'It's all right, Tilda,' Mum said, 'I've got this!'

Mum turned to the new arrival with a smile. It was a delivery driver; a man in a khaki uniform, whose face was obscured by a big parcel. He held it cradled in both arms, while he tried to wave his clipboard at Mum. 'Sign for a delivery?' he said.

'Of course,' Mum replied, and took the clipboard.

Andrew and Minnie stepped forward to help the man lower the parcel to the ground. It was about the size of a violin case and was surprisingly heavy. The driver drew the back of his hand across his forehead as he stood up. 'Thanks, it's heavy work,' he said with a smile. Andrew noticed a small scar twisted the smile out of line.

'You're welcome,' Minnie said.

The driver looked to Mum, who had not yet signed the clipboard. 'I've got a pen,' he said, reaching into his top pocket.

Mum didn't reach for it. She was looking at the man with an odd expression on her face. Lost, almost.

'Mum?' Andrew asked.

She shook herself, took the pen. 'Sorry. Sorry. A goose walked on my grave.'

She signed with a flourish.

'Thanks.' The driver headed back towards the door, then paused. He picked up a vase from a display cabinet. 'This is nice,' he said, 'how much is it?'

Mum flushed pink. 'Oh, I don't know.'

'You don't work here?' he asked, putting the vase back.

'I do. I do. I just … don't know how much that is,' Mum said; her voice shook.

Andrew caught her eye. *You're doing fine*, he tried to say. With his eyeballs.

The driver left and the bell tinkled.

Mum said nothing.

Tilda rushed in carrying a tray laden with mismatched cups and a massive teapot. 'The milk's on the turn, but it's probably OK,' she said. 'Not yoghurt, anyway. Oh, a parcel. What fun.'

She carried the tray over to a desk which was tucked into a corner and surrounded by soft chairs. There was hardly any room on the desk, as piles of papers and books and magazines formed towers, but the tray fitted neatly into one of the few places where the wood was still visible. It was obviously the place the tray lived.

'I'll leave that to brew. Let's see what's in the parcel. I'm not expecting anything, as far as I remember.'

Mum moved softly over to one of the armchairs and sank into the red velvet. Andrew glanced at her fretfully. Was she worried? About being in work, or being without him? Maybe she was just a bit tired. It had been an early start, after all.

'Minnie,' Tilda said, 'there should be some scissors on the desk. Can you pass them to me?'

The desk was a teetering pile of papers, books, old pens, a box of plasters and even a pencil sharpener shaped like a dolphin. She poked around until she saw the scissors and handed them to Tilda. Who made short work of the parcel tape and brown paper, slicing through with the blades.

A strange smell, like spices left to fade at the back of a cupboard, drifted from the discarded paper. Inside was a black box. Dark, dark wood, with silver clasps on one side and hinges on the other. Tilda flipped up the clasps and lifted the lid.

The smell was instantly stronger. With a sour note added to the spice. The lid creaked. Tilda pulled back a layer of tissue paper.

And screamed.

Chapter Two

Tilda slammed down the lid.

'What?' Minnie asked.

'What?' Andrew demanded.

'Dead thing. Used to be a cat, I think,' Tilda managed to say.

'A dead cat?' Andrew asked. 'Why did you order a dead cat?'

'I didn't!' Tilda insisted.

'Let's have a look.' Andrew dropped down to the ground beside her. Did he really want to see a dead cat? Stupid question. Of course he did. He reached for the lid.

'No!' Mum said sharply.

He looked over. She was slumped into one of the armchairs near the desk. Her bent arms formed awkward brackets on either side of her body.

'Are you all right?' Andrew asked her.

11

'Fine,' she said.

'You don't look well,' Tilda said. 'Maybe you're rushing into this? Maybe you're not quite well enough yet?'

Mum hung her head. Andrew knew that she was desperate to be able to disagree, but that Tilda was probably right. Mum was tired out just by the walk to the shop. And discouraged by not being able to answer the man's question about the vase.

She'd get there though, wouldn't she?

'If Andrew isn't allowed to look,' Minnie said, 'can I?'

Andrew was still watching Mum. Tilda was too. So Minnie reached out and lifted the lid.

The smell dragged Andrew's gaze back to the floor. 'What is that? It isn't rotting?'

'No.' Tilda pulled her silk scarf up over her nose. 'Not rotting, but still nasty.'

The tissue paper had dropped back into place. Tilda's hand hovered over the pale sheet, clearly tempted to lift it again. And Andrew considered it his duty to lead others into temptation wherever possible. 'Let's see!' he urged.

Tilda's hands lowered, almost ceremonially; she wafted the paper up, revealing the object beneath.

Ewww.

Whatever it was, it was ugly.

It was small. Cat sized. And shrivelled. And spice scented. None of its fur was visible. Instead, brown bands of intricate binding wrapped round its body. The wrappings formed triangles and diamonds where they criss-crossed. A geometry of weird. The strangest thing about it was its face. Someone had laid a mask over the space where its face would be, over the wrappings. A mouth was picked out in dark pigment. And green stones were set for its eyes.

'What is it?' Minnie asked.

'I think I know,' Tilda said. 'I've seen one in a museum. It's a mummified cat.'

'What?' Andrew asked. 'That's just weird. Who'd want to turn a cat into a mummy?' It was bizarre. Like putting clothes on an elephant. Or buying a bike for a goldfish. Just plain odd.

'Ancient Egyptians used to worship cats,' Tilda said. 'Their temples were full of them, roaming around, being serene and mysterious.'

The only cats Andrew knew were two enormous tabbies that lived in the flat upstairs. They weren't serene and mysterious. They were scabby and stinky and sprayed wee in the stairwell.

The cat in the coffin looked like an evil tenpin,

wrapped in a sitting position and laid on its back, all its legs strapped to its body.

'Can I unwrap it?' Andrew asked.

'No!' Tilda said.

'Can I touch it at least?' Andrew asked.

'No. This could be thousands of years old. There's no way anyone is touching it.'

'Tilda,' Minnie said, 'if you didn't order this, then where did it come from?'

Smash!

Their heads whipped around to where Mum was sitting. A cup lay on the ground, its handle broken off and tea spreading slowly across the wooden floorboards.

'Oh, oh, I'm so sorry!' Mum said.

There was a flurry of movement – Tilda mopping the ground with tissues, Minnie picking up broken china, and Andrew racing to Mum's side.

'Are you OK?' he asked.

'I feel a bit weak. I thought tea would help.' Her voice sounded as though it were coming from rooms away, barely there.

'I'm taking you home.'

'I'll call a taxi,' Tilda said firmly.

The strange object was, for the moment, forgotten.

Andrew let them into the flat. Mum rested the palm of her hand on the wall as she followed the corridor to her bedroom.

'I'm just going to have a catnap,' she said.

He waited outside her room, holding the door handle, while Mum lay on top of the covers and let her eyes close straight away. She still had her shoes on. That was no good. He pulled off her ballet-style pumps and set them on the floor. Then he took a rug from the back of her chair and laid it across her. Finally he drew the curtains. The light in the room turned green, like a murky pond.

Her breath had settled into the slow, even pattern of sleep.

Andrew wondered what to do with himself while Mum rested. There was an interesting recipe for baked beans and maple syrup sandwiches he'd wanted to try.

Andrew was just scraping maple syrup off the kitchen tiles when he heard Mum cry out. He dropped the sponge and ran into her room.

She was sitting up, the rug kicked to the ground, her hands held over her face.

'Mum? Mum, are you all right?'

15

She rubbed her face, lowered her hands. 'Just a bad dream. It's nothing.'

A bad dream?

Andrew felt a chill run through him, as though the bedroom really was a pond of cold water. Mum used to have a lot of bad dreams right after her accident, but they'd healed alongside her body. She hadn't had one for months now.

He sat down gently on the bed. She pulled all the pillows closer and patted the space beside her. He settled into the nest she'd made. They lay quietly for a while.

Then, 'What did you dream?' he asked.

'Fire.'

She didn't need to say anything more. A year ago she had been at work, in the florist's shop, when the fire had started. It happened fast. The firefighters thought it might have been faulty wiring, or a broken appliance, they weren't sure. But it had spread quickly. She'd tried to get out, but a ceiling had collapsed, trapping her under it. From that moment on, life had changed completely. Hospitals, doctors, specialists, physiotherapy that hurt so much it made her cry, medicines to take, appointments to keep, and remembering to do all the usual things like cooking and laundry and cleaning. Things

Andrew had become very good at. As long as you liked baked beans.

He reached out and stroked her shoulder.

'How long since you last had a bad dream?' he asked.

'A while. I suppose it's just with me going back to work. Stirred things up.' Mum shrugged. 'It was just a dream. I'm being silly. Have we got anything nice for lunch?'

'Your attempt to change the subject was terrible,' Andrew said. 'We're having beans, sort of.'

Mum laughed, but the laugh didn't last long, as though it had somewhere better to be.

'Are you sure you're OK?' Andrew asked.

'I'm fine. I'm not a case you're investigating!'

Mum pushed herself up from the bed. Andrew couldn't help wondering why Mum had said that. He hadn't even been thinking about mysteries, or investigating. Was Mum hiding something?

He would be watching her even more carefully from now on.

Chapter Three

Andrew spent the night turning and twitching, tugging his duvet up, then down, trying to sleep. But it was no use. He could almost feel Mum's unhappiness, like a damp fog in the air creeping under his door.

The first light of dawn was welcome. Might as well get up. He crept out of his room and peeped around Mum's door. She still slept.

He made some toast and ate quietly, watching the world stir beyond the flats: an early postman, someone coming home from a late night, the first workers of the day heading off to clean offices, open market stalls, cook cafe breakfasts. Morning people. He was never normally Morning People.

Neither was Mum. He'd finished breakfast and washed up before she wandered in.

'Sleep well?' he asked suspiciously.

'Like a log.'

'So, do you think you'll go back to Tilda's today?'

'No,' she said brightly. 'Not today. It's only meant to be part-time, voluntary, until I feel well enough to start looking for a proper job. After yesterday, I don't want to rush it.'

Her eyes sparkled with a frantic energy.

Andrew didn't like it. But he forced himself not to say anything. Well, almost nothing. Hardly anything. 'But you do want to go back sometime? You didn't have any more nightmares? You feel all right? Or not? Do I need to call a doctor or the physio? Do you want an appointment today?'

Mum raised her hands at the onslaught of questions. 'Wait! Wait!'

But she was saved from answering by the sudden trill of the phone in the hallway.

They looked at each other. A staring stand-off.

The phone kept ringing.

Andrew broke first. 'I'll get it!' He grabbed the receiver. 'Yes?' he said.

'And good morning to you too!' Minnie's voice.

'Sorry. Morning.'

'Listen, something … interesting has happened on Marsh Road.'

'Gossip?' Andrew loved gossip. Celebrity gossip was the best, but market gossip would do too. 'Go on,' he said.

'Well, this morning, just when the market traders were setting up, Tilda came out to open the shop shutters. Anyway, next thing anyone knew, she was screaming!'

'Screaming? Why?' Andrew gripped the receiver tighter. There was way too much screaming going on for his liking these last twenty-four hours.

'No one knows. She yelled blue murder, then ran straight back into her shop and slammed the door behind her. No one's seen her since.'

'Have you called Flora?' Andrew said.

'No.'

'I think you should. There's something weird going on. And it isn't just my cooking.'

'You think there's a mystery?'

'Well, my mum had a nightmare yesterday, and she won't go to work this morning. Which doesn't seem to matter because the place she's meant to be working at hasn't even opened its doors because the owner was yelling in the street.'

'Oh. Is your mum OK?'

'She will be, I'll make sure of it. You call Flora. I'll get Piotr. We'll be there in fifteen minutes.'

'A mummified cat,' Flora said fifteen minutes later in Marsh Road cafe. 'I wish you'd called us. I'd have loved to see it.' She crossed her arms and dropped her chin. If it were her twin sister, Sylvie, Andrew would have supposed that she was sulking. But Flora wasn't Sylvie.

Sylvie was definitely sulking. 'We never get to see the good stuff!' she said, sticking out her bottom lip.

'That's not true!' Minnie said. 'Flora tried the Breeze 5000 before anyone else, and you got kidnapped by art smugglers!' Minnie was referring to old cases they'd solved.

'It's not a mummified cat though, is it?' Sylvie said.

'The cat's probably still there,' Piotr said, trying to cheer everyone up. 'I didn't get to see it either. But I'm sure Tilda will let us look, if we ask.'

'No she won't,' Sylvie said. 'The shop was all locked up when we walked past. No sign of Tilda at all. Whatever it was that gave her the screaming habdabs this morning hasn't worn off. If you ask me, I think she was drunk.'

Minnie gave her a pot-plant-withering stare. 'No she was not. There's something odd going on. Think about it.

Tilda takes delivery of a creepy cat. Then loses her new employee. And seems to lose it in the street.'

'Is it a case, though?' Flora asked.

'It could be,' Minnie replied. 'I've got a feeling.'

That seemed to satisfy Flora. She was smiling a full Pollyanna smile, her freckles dotting her apple cheeks. 'Then this seems like the perfect time to buy a new notebook!' she said. She rifled in her backpack for a second before pulling out her purse; then she raced over to the second-hand book stall. They also sold blank notebooks, of the sort she loved for keeping their discoveries straight.

Was Minnie right? Was there a mystery here? Or was it just coincidence that Tilda and Mum were behaving oddly at the same time? Was Mum just overtired by trying to go back to work too soon? Andrew didn't think it was a coincidence. His mystery sense was tingling.

It wasn't long before Flora was back. She'd picked out a notebook with a gold and purple cover. It looked like a good place to store strange goings-on.

'First things first,' Piotr said. 'We need to talk to Tilda to see what she was so scared of. Where did she go after you saw her?' he asked Minnie.

'Into the shop.'

'Let's see if she'll let us in.'

They left the cafe and strolled past Minnie's mum's salon. They stopped outside Meeke and Sons Curios and Gimcracks. Andrew had no idea what a gimcrack was, but he wanted one.

The dark glass in the shop window was unlit. The usual trays of battered cutlery, mismatched crockery and weird Victorian curling irons were missing from outside the shop. It looked as though it had been abandoned. This impression wasn't helped by the fact that Tilda had never repainted the old sign that curled and flaked above the door like the wood had dandruff.

'Is she in there?' Flora said doubtfully.

Minnie went to the door and tried the handle. Locked. She rang the bell. They heard its timorous trill somewhere deep inside the shop.

Nothing.

And then, movement.

A shadow at the back of the shop scurried like something afraid of the light. It got closer. Andrew pressed his face up to the glass so that he could see better. Tilda. Her head was stooped, her shoulders hunched up to her ears. She was a tight packet of a person. She paused and flashed a look at the door, before rushing over to open it.

'Tilda, are you OK?' Minnie asked.

'Fine.' She held on to the door with both hands, not opening it enough to allow them in.

'Well,' Minnie said slowly. 'I was a bit worried. We all were. Because you seemed not really fine outside earlier …'

Tilda leaned out of the shop doorway, just a fraction, and glanced quickly up and down the street.

Andrew had no idea what she was looking for, but whatever is was, it apparently wasn't there, because Tilda stepped back into the shop and pulled the door open just enough for them all to slip inside.

It was cold inside the shop after the bright sunshine of the street. Andrew wrapped his arms around his middle. It took a moment too for his eyes to get used to the dark. The piles of stuff made it difficult for the light to get in. Green and purple spots floated in his vision for a while.

He stepped forward and hoped he wouldn't barge into anything too valuable.

Tilda led them towards the counter. Then she dropped into the wooden chair beside it as though the weight of the world were pushing her down. 'I don't know what to do,' she said.

'How about you tell us what happened?' Piotr said.

'I don't know. You won't believe me. No one will, not even children.'

'Try us,' Piotr said.

Tilda shook her head. 'What happened today was a silly old woman imagining things.'

'What things? You can trust us,' Piotr said.

'Well,' Tilda said uncertainly.

'Please?' Flora tucked her pencil away; notes could be made later.

Tilda sighed. 'I was opening up the shop. It was a lovely morning, bright and sunny. I'd planned on nipping to the veg stall to get some nice tomatoes for lunch. But then I saw it …' Tilda's hands creased around a handkerchief in her lap.

'Saw what?' Andrew asked.

'A bright flash, and then, the Eye of Ra,' Tilda whispered.

They all looked at each other with looks more blank than Flora's notebook.

'What does that mean?' Sylvie asked.

Tilda twisted the knot of fabric in her palms and shook her head. 'I must have been imagining things. But it seemed so real, so solid.'

'What is the Eye of Ra?' Andrew asked impatiently. Minnie shot him a look.

'An ancient symbol,' Tilda said. 'It comes from Egypt.

It's a representation of the god Ra. It's drawn as an eye, outlined in thick black eye make-up. It was used as a violent charm, to ward off evil by causing pain and destruction.'

Andrew felt the skin on his arms tighten into goose-bumps. He wasn't a fan of violent charms. Especially not angry ancient-god ones. He gripped his elbows and glanced at the dark floor, at the shadows. He wondered what an ancient, evil charm might get up to.

'When you say you saw it,' Piotr said, 'what did you mean, exactly?'

Tilda looked towards the window. Outside the sunshine splattered Marsh Road in cheetah-coat patterns, speckling the stalls and the surface of the street.

Inside, in the dark, Andrew still watched the shadows.

'It was there,' Tilda pointed, 'on the glass, like it was hovering in front of it. An apparition. It was transparent, ghostly. And it was big too; it filled the frame. It just came from nowhere. It was looking right at me. I felt an icy hand squeezing at my heart. I just screamed. I couldn't help it. As soon as I opened my mouth, the Eye disappeared.'

Andrew moved over to the glass. It looked perfectly ordinary. A bit grimy in places maybe, the dust of the street gathering in small peaks along the outside sill. But no sign of a spectral shape, or strange symbol.

Flora stood beside him, eyeing the glass keenly. 'It might have been some kind of optical illusion,' she said softly. 'She might just have seen something reflected on the dark glass.'

'What about the icy hands? The squozen heart?'

Flora shrugged. 'It's too soon to be sure about anything.' She turned to the counter and held out her notebook. 'Do you think you could draw the Eye of Ra?'

Tilda nodded. She took the book and began to sketch quickly. She scribbled out a few lines, tried again and then handed the notebook back. 'Here. It's quite a simple shape, but was once considered one of the most powerful symbols on earth.'

Flora looked at the sheet, then passed it around.

'Wait!' Minnie said. 'I think I've seen this before!' Her eyes scanned the gloomy space. 'Where's the cat? The mummy we saw yesterday?'

Tilda stood up. She shuffled across the room towards a big dresser; the black wood was stained with age and patterns had been cut into its knots and whorls, faces emerging from the timber. 'I put it in here, for safekeeping until someone claims it.'

27

She lifted the heavy bundle from the shelf and carried it over to the counter.

Minnie leaned in close and peered at the dark wooden casing. It was scratched and battered with age. She clicked the clasps and raised the lid gently. In a cobra move, she dipped side to side, examining the cat from every angle.

Then she reached into the case and very gently, very carefully, moved aside the tissue paper and lifted the cat. Andrew gasped and looked at Tilda – would she object? No, she seemed so dazed, the fact that Minnie was touching the tabby didn't seem to register.

'There!' Minnie said, standing it upright. 'I knew I'd seen it.' She pointed at its bound chest. The bandages formed a tight chevron pattern, but marked faintly, in a worn grey, was the Eye.

'That was it!' Tilda said. 'That was it exactly!'

Everyone else gathered around the cat. Flora peering in for a closer look; Sylvie sniffing with disgust; Minnie and Piotr careful but curious.

Andrew still wanted to unwrap it.

'There's something else in here,' Flora said. She reached into the case and lifted out a folded sheet of paper. It had yellowed with age and wear; along the folds it was as thin as fabric. Flora was gentle as she opened it.

Andrew looked over her shoulder.

It was a handwritten letter on a small sheet of paper. A black-and-white line drawing in the top right showed a Sphinx's head, under which was printed Cairo Hotel. The note itself was hard to read, the handwriting was joined-up and loopy, but Flora read aloud to the others.

'"Dear Sirs, A further specimen for your collection. Pay no heed to the tall tales of the diggers. No gentleman fears a curse. Payment on delivery, as agreed." I can't read the signature, it's way too squiggly.'

A curse?

A curse?

Gentlemen might not fear curses. Andrew guessed this meant he wasn't a gentleman.

Flora held the letter up towards the light. 'There's a watermark on the paper. It's faded and worn. But I can make out a word that begins with "V" and ends in "y".'

'Very?' Sylvie suggested. 'Victory? Verity?'

'Valley,' Tilda said from her chair. 'Is it Valley?'

'It might be,' Flora agreed.

'Valley of the Kings,' Tilda said. 'It's where Egyptian

pharaohs were buried. With their treasures. And their pets.'

They all looked at the cat. 'Poor Tibbles,' Minnie muttered.

'Poor Tibbles?' Andrew exclaimed. 'Poor Tibbles? That cat is cursed! The Eye of Ra appeared this morning. Tilda is terrified. Mum's having nightmares again. Who knows what might happen next. We all might die in our beds. Or have our teeth fall out!'

Flora folded the note and laid it carefully back in the box. 'Andrew, there's no such thing as curses.'

Andrew glanced back at Tilda, whose pale fingers gripped the edge of her chair. Even the bright clothes and bold jewellery couldn't disguise how ashen she looked. Tilda, at this moment, reminded Andrew of a circus tent left out in a storm. 'How do you explain that, then?' he hissed, gesturing at Tilda.

'I can't. Yet,' Flora said. 'But whatever's going on, we're going to get to the bottom of it.'

Chapter Four

Flora spent a long time pacing outside Meeke and Sons, checking the window, pulling down the shutters, pushing them back up again. She was checking for clues, anything that looked as though it didn't belong. But she put her notebook away without recording anything. 'There's nothing there,' she said. 'If there was a ghostly apparition, there's no sign of it now.'

Andrew surveyed the road: bustling market traders, the smell of fruit and flowers, the air a little hazy with dust from the building site across the way. It all looked normal. Had Tilda really seen the Eye of Ra?

'Come on,' Piotr said, 'let's get a doughnut and think about it.'

They settled into their usual seat near the window of the cafe while Piotr fetched snacks. He cut the doughnut into four (Sylvie didn't want extra sugar today) and handed out the pieces.

Andrew eyed the red gloop oozing from the dough and pooling on the pale plate. 'A curse in Marsh Road,' he said.

'It's not a curse,' Flora said. She popped her portion into her mouth without getting any sugar on her face, and chewed.

'How do you explain what Tilda saw, then? And how scared she was? And –' Andrew paused, then decided he had to say something '– and how weird Mum's been since that stupid cat turned up.'

'How weird?' Minnie asked.

'Tired. Sad. Having bad dreams again. All the things I thought were over.' He shrugged.

'You should eat that,' Piotr said. 'It will make you feel better.'

Andrew doubted that very much. Could a quarter of a doughnut counteract the effects of an ancient curse that had settled over them like a rain cloud of doom? He ate it anyway, just in case. The dusting of sugar crunched under his teeth. The jam tasted of summer strawberries. Maybe, in future, he should listen to Piotr.

In future.

That was it!

He made a noise that was part squeal, part gulp.

Minnie reached to slap his back, but he waved her off. He wasn't choking. He was having a brilliant idea. And perhaps choking a little bit.

Once the spluttering was over, and the doughnut was successfully swallowed, Andrew was able to speak again. 'Fortune teller! There's a fortune teller in the market. She must know all about curses. Isn't it the same kind of thing? Like, if you can do one, you can do the other? I definitely know she sells lucky charms.'

'Andrew,' Flora said, raising her voice slightly, 'just because someone sells plastic four-leaf clovers on a market stall doesn't mean they know about two-thousand-year-old ancient curses. Especially when there's no such thing as two-thousand-year-old ancient curses.'

Andrew brushed the sugar from his fingertips. 'Flora, you don't realise how lucky we are. There's an actual psychic not a hundred metres away from this very cafe. My mum is plagued by nightmares and Tilda is haunted by visions. And we have absolutely no clues at all. We should take this chance to get an expert opinion on events.'

The busy cafe was full of the sound of clattering

33

cups and chattering people. Frying eggs and bacon sizzled; the scents of cooking vied with the tang of spray cleaners and soap. It was all so normal. None of these customers knew about the weight of the curse which had dropped like a winter duvet over the junk shop two doors down. *Poor, innocent fools*, Andrew thought sadly.

'I'm not going to ask a charlatan in a shawl to solve this case for us!' Flora said hotly.

'What's a charlatan?' Piotr asked.

'A fraud, a phoney! We need some good solid leads and some good solid detective work to get those leads. Not some random wild goose chase.'

How could talking to a fortune teller be a wild goose chase? They were paid to give you answers! But before Andrew could object, Sylvie spoke.

'What exactly would a good, solid lead in a case about a mummified cat look like?' she asked.

Flora flushed a little. 'I'm not sure. I don't know what we're dealing with. Something made Tilda think she saw the Eye of Ra. And it's too much of a coincidence that it happened just after an Egyptian artefact arrived. But whatever it is, it isn't a curse. Is it, Piotr?' She looked at Piotr for backup.

34

There was no use looking at him – he'd be on Andrew's side!

'Well,' Piotr said. 'I think it would be interesting to know where exactly the cat came from. And I don't mean Egypt. I mean Tilda didn't order it, didn't know anything about it. So why did it arrive at the shop? You guys were there. Who delivered it and where from?'

Oh.

Piotr wasn't on Andrew's side.

Andrew slumped down in his seat and looked out of the window. He could just make out the red-and-white-striped tent of the fortune teller, tucked in neatly among the other stalls.

Someone said something about the delivery driver.

He wondered how much it would cost to have a reading with the psychic.

Minnie said something about clipboards.

Maybe the fortune teller would do them a deal when she heard about the curse?

'Andrew!' Piotr was shouting his name.

'What?'

'Concentrate. Can you remember anything about the delivery driver? Any detail that might help us find him?'

Andrew sighed deeply, and dragged his eyes away from the market back to the cafe table. 'He was just a guy. I don't know.'

'Well, neither do we,' Minnie said. 'I can't believe I didn't even look at him! Can you remember anything at all?'

'He was a white guy. And pretty tall.'

'Great. That narrows it down,' Sylvie said, dripping sarcasm all over her napkin.

'I hadn't finished.' Andrew glared. 'He was a white guy, and tall, *and* he had a small scar, on his top lip.'

There was a pause at the table. Flora piled their empty plates up, ready to go back to the counter. 'That's not bad,' she said finally, 'but I don't know if we can find him just from that. Maybe your mum might remember better?'

Andrew shook his head firmly. 'We're not bothering her. She's not feeling well.'

'Tilda, then,' Flora said.

'I'm not going off on a *wild goose chase* looking for a man with a scar, when we've got a perfectly good lead right there in the market,' Andrew said.

Flora stood up and lifted the plates. 'Fine. No one's stopping you. But you're doing it yourself.'

'No, I'm not. Piotr will come with me, won't you, Piotr?'

Piotr raised his hands in defeat. 'Yes, all right, I'll come with you.'

'In the meantime, we'll get on with proper interviewing,' Flora said.

Andrew had no idea how he had started this row, but he knew he was on the right path. And he was going to prove it.

Chapter Five

Andrew and Piotr watched the girls leave. Only Minnie glanced back and gave him a sympathetic look. Flora and Sylvie were set on finding the delivery driver, not gazing into crystal balls.

He'd show them.

Andrew pushed his glasses up his nose, ready for action.

They both stood and headed for the door. Andrew led the way, sure that his best friend was at his back.

The market buzzed with the sound of shoppers and traders and just passing-through-ers. Andrew weaved his way through, glancing back now and again to make sure Piotr's mousy hair bobbed behind him. Now that they were getting closer to the fortune teller, he felt slightly less confident. A bit more, well, frightened. What if she told them terrible things about the future? What if she said he was never going to be a star? Never going to be in films? Or on telly? Or even be the host of a local radio show?

He wiped his palms against the front of his jeans.

He mentally gave himself a shake. This was ridiculous. He had nothing to be scared of. His future was bright. Everyone said so. Even teachers, when they weren't telling him off.

They were at the tent.

It wasn't an easy-build pop-up style. It was made of proper canvas, with ropes and poles attached to heavy weights to anchor it. If he squinted, he could imagine a knight in armour stepping out of it, ready to joust. The door flapped a little in the breeze and the air around it smelled of burning incense. It made his nose itch.

'Ready?' Piotr asked.

'Let's do it.'

Andrew pulled back the fabric door and stepped inside. Immediately he was struck by the gloom, the shadows. A second layer of purple fabric lined the inside of the tent. It took a moment for his eyes to adjust. Pinpricks of bright light seeped in from tiny tears in the purple, like stars shining in the night sky. And there was a small lamp on a table in the centre of the tent casting an orange glow. The lamp battled bravely but fruitlessly with the shadows.

Two green eyes flashed, low to the ground. Andrew nearly yelped. Then he felt soft fur, warm, weaving its way in a figure of eight around his ankles. The fortune teller's cat. Phew.

A voice came, whispering, from a dark corner. 'Who comes to seek the wisdom of Elspeth?'

Andrew looked at Piotr. He could make out the moon-pale skin of his face, but his dark jumper blended against the purple background, making his head look disembodied. Severed.

Andrew gulped. 'Err, hi, how are you? We, err, that is, we … I'm Andrew, this is Piotr. And I guess we've come to seek wisdom. Or at least, to find stuff out. If that's the same thing.'

The woman chuckled. 'A babbler, I see.'

There was the sound of rustling silks, then the smell of tobacco and spice, and the woman stepped forward. Elspeth was short, almost as short as Andrew and definitely not as tall as Piotr. It was hard to make out much more until she reached the pool of light cast by the lamp. She sat down at the table. Her face was lined, but her hair was still jet-black. Her clothes, like the inside of the tent, were black-and-purple drapes, layered over her body in billowing folds.

Andrew was impressed at how fortune-tellery she was managing to look. She could help – then Flora would see.

She scooped up the cat. It was dark as midnight and its strong purr was hypnotic. Elspeth waved them forward and they sat on the cushions she indicated. Andrew sank down quickly, surprised at just how wobbly his knees were feeling. It must be the incense. It was bound to make him light-headed. He gripped his hands into fists.

'Seeking your fortunes, boys?' Elspeth asked. She raised a dark eyebrow and a smile curled on her red lips. 'That will be two pounds.'

'Not my fortune,' Andrew managed to say. His mouth was strangely dry and his tongue stuck uncomfortably to the roof of his mouth. 'Advice, we need advice.'

'Interesting,' said Elspeth. The word was breathed like a secret. 'What do you need advice about?'

'You'd think she'd know,' Piotr whispered, very unhelpfully Andrew thought.

'I heard that,' Elspeth said sharply.

'Sorry,' Piotr said, dropping his head and breaking her gaze.

'I can only see the future when I spread the tarot cards,

or bring about a trance-like state,' Elspeth said, sounding quite grumpy. 'It doesn't happen just by looking at you. So, why don't you tell me why you're here and stop wasting my time?'

'Sorry,' Piotr said again.

'Do you know anything about curses?' Andrew asked quickly, before she could get worked up.

'Setting them or lifting them? Setting them costs more.'

'Lifting. Definitely lifting.'

'It depends. Some curses can be very powerful, very dangerous. Others are like annoying puppies; they get under your feet, but they're pretty harmless. Wait. Let me see the nature of what we're dealing with.'

She pushed the cat off her lap. It dropped to the floor with a disgruntled mewl and then was lost to the shadows. Elspeth lifted a dark cloth from the floor. As she unwrapped it, Andrew saw that it swaddled a deck of cards. Tarot cards. They looked old, bent and scored by time. 'Cut the deck,' Elspeth instructed, placing the cards in front of Andrew. He did as he was told. The papery edges of the cards felt fragile against his fingertips. 'Now, deal five cards, face up.'

He turned the first card. A woman sat on a throne. The

faded colours had once been red and green and gold, but were now pink and blue and yellow.

'The Empress,' Elspeth said. 'A strong woman. Your mummy?'

'What?' How could she know?

'Your mother perhaps?'

He turned the next card. His skin pricked into goose-bumps. A man stood on a chariot. The chariot was being pulled by two black-and-white sphinxes in Egyptian headdresses.

The next card. A lion.

'Strength,' Elspeth whispered. 'Strength returns after an arduous journey.'

The fourth card. Two dogs howling at the moon.

'But the strength has become confusion. Darkness draws close.'

The last card.

Andrew's hand shook as he laid it on the table. A man hung, by his feet, from a gallows.

'The Hanged Man,' Elspeth whispered. 'Not always as bad as it looks.' Her laugh was not entirely kind.

'What does it mean?' Andrew asked. 'Is it really about my mother?'

Elspeth stared at him for a moment. It felt as though

she was unwrapping each layer of his skin, staring right into the heart of him.

Then she spoke. 'Your mother is poorly, yes? You need to know what to do for her?'

'Sort of,' Andrew agreed. 'She was getting better. But then the cat arrived.'

'The cat? Ah.' Elspeth tapped the card with the lion roaring on it. 'This cat?'

'No, it's a real cat. Well, a mummified one. With a curse on it.'

Piotr nudged him suddenly, catching an elbow right in Andrew's rib. He gasped and glared at his friend.

'Your friend is worried that you speak too much,' Elspeth said. 'He is probably right. You seem to be a talker. But in this instance you can tell me nothing that the cards don't already say.'

'Is there a curse then?' Andrew leaned forward, his hands clasped around his ribs to guard against Piotr's elbows. 'Can we lift it?'

'The cards say yes, and maybe. All was well, until this sudden change. Whether you can change the course of the chariot depends on how well you can listen.'

Andrew's heart sank a little. His report cards always said 'needs to listen as well as talk'.

'At the point where day becomes night –' Elspeth held a painted finger above the picture of the moon '– at twilight, that is when the curse is at its strongest. If you can find out why the curse was set, perhaps you can lift it. You need to listen to the voices of the void.'

'How exactly do we do that?' Piotr asked.

'Simply by paying attention. If the voices want to be heard, then they will speak to you. At dusk. When the veil is thin. Right. That will be three pounds.'

'You said two!' Piotr protested.

'Cursed cats is extra,' Elspeth said firmly.

Andrew paid up, and Elspeth tidied away the cards, back under their cloth cover.

'Be careful,' she said, as they left the tent, 'curses are dangerous, remember.'

From the shadows, her cat hissed.

Chapter Six

Minnie, Flora and Sylvie left the cafe and headed back towards Tilda's. Part of Minnie wished that she could have gone to the fortune teller too; the striped canvas looked like something from a fairy story. But Flora was right, what they needed were cold hard facts – and a good lead on the delivery driver. He was definitely real, at least.

'It's funny that Andrew spotted the driver's scar, but you didn't,' Sylvie said.

'Hilarious,' Minnie said.

'It's good he remembered,' Flora said, stepping between Sylvie and Minnie. 'It gives us somewhere to start. And maybe Tilda will remember more.'

Inside the cool cave of a shop, Tilda was on the phone. She cupped her palm around the black, old-fashioned receiver, but they could still make out what she was saying. 'Yes, that would be best … I don't know … how long could you stay?' Tilda raised her hand in a wave as they filed in. 'I've got visitors … yes, visitors, not customers. I'll see you soon. Bye.' She hung up.

'Everything all right?' Minnie asked.

'My nephew. Worrying over nothing.' Tilda waved at the phone. But although she was trying to sound fine, Minnie had the feeling that underneath she was still frightened.

'He's coming to see you?' Minnie asked.

Tilda nodded. 'He's just going to pop in. He heard about the, well, kerfuffle, and he wants to check. I told him I was fine, but he wouldn't take no for an answer.'

Minnie stepped closer and rested a hand on Tilda's arm. Tilda dropped her own hand on Minnie's. It felt cold and clammy.

They had to help Tilda. She was too nice to feel frightened in her own shop. It wasn't fair.

'We've got a plan,' Minnie said firmly. 'We're going to try and find the delivery driver and then see if he knows where the cat came from. If we know more about the cat, then we might be able to explain what happened to you.'

'That's kind of you, girls,' Tilda said.

Flora rummaged in her bag until she found her notebook. 'We were wondering whether you could remember anything about the delivery driver who brought the cat?'

Tilda's hands cradled across her chest. 'It's nice that you want to help. But this is a bad business. You shouldn't get involved. I'd hate for any of you to be hurt.'

'Why would we get hurt looking for a delivery driver?' Flora asked.

'Not the driver. The curse. I don't want to drag you into anything.'

'Well,' Sylvie said, 'as I understand it, Minnie was here when you opened the parcel. She passed you a pair of scissors, which makes her an accomplice as far as the curse is concerned. She is involved.'

Flora tutted at her twin.

Minnie felt a sudden shiver. Was Sylvie right? She hadn't thought of that before.

Tilda's eyes fell on Minnie and Minnie was horrified to realise that there was pity there. Tilda believed she was cursed too!

'Minnie is not cursed,' Flora said sharply. 'And neither are you. But there is something strange going on. With no clues at the scene, the next best thing is to find this driver. He'll be able to tell us where the parcel came from, who paid for it, things like that.'

'I suppose that would be OK. As long as you were careful,' Tilda said slowly. 'But how will you find him?'

'I don't suppose you remember which company he was from?' Flora asked. 'We know what he looks like – well, more or less – so once we know his company, then it should be easy to find who he is.'

Tilda looked at the piles of paper on her desk. She traced her fingers along a precariously balanced tower of letters and bills and receipts. 'Did I get a delivery note, I wonder?'

She pulled randomly at some envelopes and, like autumn leaves, they fluttered to the floor.

Minnie bent to help collect them. Tilda's system was so chaotic! How did she ever find anything? Mum didn't run the salon like this. She filed every bill, every receipt, and knew exactly what was happening in the business. Tilda probably didn't know whether the shop made any money or not!

'I don't think I did sign anything,' Tilda said fretfully. 'I don't remember.'

'Andrew's mum signed,' Minnie said. 'But he doesn't want us to ask her.' She saw Sylvie tilt her head thoughtfully. Obviously wondering why Andrew didn't want them following a lead.

'How about the wrapping?' Flora asked. 'There might have been a company label on it.'

'It's in the bin,' Tilda said.

Sylvie inched over to the wastepaper bin under Tilda's desk. It was jammed full of rubbish – cellophane, paper, yoghurt pots and apple cores. Sylvie wrinkled her nose up at it. 'This?' she asked.

'Yup,' Minnie replied. 'Go on, see if you can find it. It was plain brown paper.'

Sylvie's wrinkled nose became a wrinkled brow, chin, mouth as she lowered her hand into the bin.

'It's like a tombola, but with rubbish!' Minnie said, helpfully.

'Eww!' Sylvie complained. But she pulled out the brown paper. It was scrunched and a bit stained, but it was definitely the right one.

Flora took it from her sister and unfolded it gently, smoothing out the creases. 'That's weird,' she said.

'What?'

'There's just the address label. No stamps. Or marks of any kind. No return address or delivery barcode. Nothing.'

'So?' Sylvie was still looking ruffled. Minnie wished she'd thought to take a picture of Sylvie with her hand in the bin. Next time.

'When parcels come to our house to be signed, they've got all kinds of things on them so that people can track their deliveries. It's odd. One more odd thing in a line of odd things.'

'Do you know what it means?' Sylvie asked.

'It means,' Minnie replied, 'that there's no way of knowing which delivery company the driver works for. Not unless we call every single one of them in the world and describe the driver.'

Sylvie held out her hands. 'So I rummaged in the bin for nothing? Great! I think I must be cursed too.'

'There's no curse,' Flora said, a little crossly.

'But we're no closer to finding the driver?' Sylvie asked.

Flora looked down at the plain brown paper on the ground. 'We've got nothing,' she said.

Chapter Seven

'I've got something!' Andrew said, waving his arms above his head. The girls, who were standing outside Meeke's, hadn't noticed him. 'Oi!' he yelled over the sound of shoppers and traders and hammers from the building site. 'I've got something!'

He raced up to them, with Piotr striding quickly behind. He sensed a gloom, a despondency, a very strong Lack of Clues hanging over them. He'd cheer them up. 'I've got something!' he said again.

Flora's hands flew to her ears. 'No need to yell!'

'Is it from the fortune teller?' Minnie asked.

'Yup,' Andrew said.

'Come and tell us,' Minnie said.

There was a bench in the window of her mum's salon next door. There were no customers, so Minnie led them inside. Bernice, her mum's assistant, was using a broom as

52

a microphone, singing along to the radio, as they went in. She raised her hand, but didn't stop singing.

Andrew dropped into the window seat first. He felt the news from Elspeth fizz inside him, waiting to pop out like a champagne cork. The others sat beside him, or pulled stools closer.

'So,' Minnie said, 'what did the fortune teller say?'

'We need to find out what the cat wants,' Andrew said.

'The *dead* cat?' Flora asked.

'Yes. We need to listen to it at twilight. If we listen hard enough, when the – what was it, Piotr?'

'The veil between worlds.'

'Yes, that. When that's thin, at twilight, we'll hear what it wants. Then we can lift the curse.'

Andrew grinned at the others. But it was odd. The cloud they'd been under didn't seem to have lifted at all.

'Andrew,' Flora said gently, 'that cat died millennia ago. It had its internal organs removed and replaced with oil and natron. I know, we did Egyptians in school.'

'Eww,' Minnie said.

Flora nodded in agreement. 'Eww, yes. But also, that cat hasn't wanted anything in a very long time.'

Andrew leaned back against the window. He hadn't realised how annoying Flora could be before. It was almost as though she didn't want to believe. He forced himself to look away, to calm down, to count to ten, to try to make an anagram from the signs he could see. But there were no interesting words in 'Vasey Construction, no accidents in 47 days' or 'Marsh Road News and Off-Licence'. And he was still cross when he got to ten.

'Bernice!' he yelled. 'Do you believe in curses?'

Bernice stopped singing into the broom handle. 'What?'

'Do you think curses are real?'

'I've felt a bit cursed before now. On days when a delivery doesn't arrive and a gas bill does.'

'But really, really cursed?' Andrew pressed.

'I always salute a magpie if I see one on its own. I can't help myself. And my nana always said bad things came in threes. But those are superstitions, aren't they? Not curses. I don't know, where would a curse come from?'

'My cousins told me that witch doctors can put curses on people,' Minnie said, remembering a long-ago trip to Lagos.

'And wicked fairies are always cursing princesses,' Sylvie added, remembering some beloved Disney DVDs.

'And witches curse anyone who tries to steal their cow,' Piotr said, remembering a collection of folk tales his mum had read to him and Kasia.

Now it was Flora's turn to glare at the window.

Bernice grinned and swirled the broom about her legs like a dance partner. 'Sounds like a good case!' She sailed towards the back of the shop, singing again.

'So, we listen to the cat tonight? At twilight?' Andrew said. 'I've got to get home to make sure Mum's all right, so it can't be too late.'

Sylvie leaned in a little closer. 'Listen,' she said, 'why don't we just ask your mum whether she remembers any more about the delivery driver than you lot do? I know you don't want to, but why? I don't get it.'

Andrew felt the excitement drain like water from a leaky bucket.

It was his job to keep Mum safe, even from nightmares. 'I don't want to go bothering her,' he said. 'She won't remember. She was hardly even looking at him.'

'But,' Sylvie said, 'she signed the paperwork; she might have noticed a logo, or something.'

Andrew thought about Mum waking up in the night, crying out. She didn't need him coming in asking her questions, frightening her with this curse. 'No,' he said. 'We can't trace the driver. We go after the cat.'

He caught a look that Piotr gave Minnie. 'What?'

'Nothing,' Piotr said. 'We go after the cat.'

'Good.'

But it didn't feel good. It felt like everyone was thinking something they didn't want to say out loud, and that was his fault.

He'd brought everyone down, so it was his job to cheer them all up again. Andrew leaped up from the bench, he grabbed a fat, round brush from in front of a mirror and held it to his mouth. 'Ladies and gentlemen,' he said with a flourish. 'Tonight, as the clock strikes seven, the magical mystical hour of seven – think seven dwarfs, seven dancing princesses, seven … err … swans a swimming – we will be found, waiting for dusk, the moment when day becomes night, inside Meeke and Sons Curios and Gimcracks, waiting for the curse of the mummy to reveal itself. Ready to listen to the voice of the netherworld. Who's with me?'

Piotr whooped and punched the air. Even Sylvie laughed.

Andrew gave the softest sigh. They were on his side again.

'Fine, fine.' Flora held up her hands in defeat. 'We'll be there.'

Chapter Eight

At a quarter to seven, Andrew checked in on Mum, who was curled up on the sofa reading a book. He could leave her for a while. He headed into the soft evening light, towards Meeke's. He called for Piotr on the way, and they both stopped in for Minnie.

Sylvie and Flora were already inside the shop. Tilda had let them in. But the three weren't alone.

There was a man in the shop too. Andrew could tell right away that he was part of the next generation of Meekes. Not only did he look quite meek, the sort of person who might just inherit the earth, if no one stamped on him before he got to the front of the queue, but also he had Tilda's jaw, the exact same face shape, as though he were a blurry photocopy of Tilda.

He had dirty-blond, wispy hair, and not quite enough of it to cover his entire head. His suit jacket was creased and worn to shininess at the elbows. He looked a little nervous at the sudden appearance of the gang.

'This is Benedict,' Sylvie said. 'Tilda's nephew. He just got here. Benedict, this is Piotr, and the others.'

'Minnie,' Minnie said sharply, 'and Andrew.'

Andrew held out his hand. Benedict looked surprised, but held out his own to be shaken. His palm was damp – it reminded Andrew of pulling off football socks after PE class. This shaking hands business wasn't all it was cracked up to be.

Benedict gave a squirrelish nod, then pulled back his hands and let his fingers twitch across his lapels, dislodging a few dog hairs as he did so. 'Are you really going to leave these youngsters alone here, Aunt Tilda? Is that wise?'

'Don't you think I should?'

'Well, no. I'm here now, and whatever it is that's worrying you, I can help you with it.' Benedict leaned against the desk, resting on a few centimetres of clear space. He picked up a glass paperweight and passed it from one hand to the other. 'If you need me, I'm always here, you know that.'

'I do,' Tilda replied. 'But this whole business has been very trying, and these children have been remarkably kind.'

'Trying how?'

There was a moment of silence, as everyone looked to someone else to begin the explanation. Andrew opened his mouth, but Piotr shook his head, so Andrew closed it again.

Tilda walked over to the shelf and lifted down the black case. 'Yesterday, a curse arrived, delivered inside a mummy. A cat. I opened the lid and let it out. Now it's here and I don't know how to get rid of it.' She described the Eye of Ra in a halting voice.

'I'm sorry, Aunt Tilda, but I'm afraid you're not making any sense.'

'Look inside,' she said.

He lifted the lid, pulled aside the tissue, and gawped. His mouth hung open and his eyebrows took a high jump. 'Is that real?' he asked. 'A real mummy? Is it valuable?'

'I have no idea,' Tilda said. 'I expect so. Look at the letter.' She helped him pull free the note they'd read. He scanned it, then dropped it back on top of the tissue paper.

'So, let me get this straight,' he said. 'You think that a haunted cat has brought a curse to Meeke's Curios?' His voice rose at the end of his sentence as he struggled to keep a grip on his feelings.

'That's it exactly,' Tilda said.

'I need to sit down,' Benedict gasped. He pushed back on to the desk, forcing a clatter of objects to spill over the far side. Tilda winced at the noise, but said nothing. She lowered the lid and put the mummy back on the shelf.

Benedict wheezed uncomfortably.

'Do you need a glass of water?' Tilda asked.

Benedict didn't reply. He was pulling sharply at his tie. He loosened the knot and yanked his collar.

'Sweetheart?' Tilda said. 'Are you unwell?'

Nothing.

'I think Benedict might need something a little stronger than water,' Sylvie said.

'Aunt … Aunt …' Benedict struggled to speak.

Tilda nodded. 'You're right. I have some brandy at home. I'll take him there.'

'Aunt Tilda, this is preposterous!' Benedict finally managed to say.

'But brandy is an excellent idea,' Tilda said.

'Not the brandy! The curse! The whole thing is barking.' Benedict pressed his fingers to his temples. He appeared to be mentally counting to ten.

'Benedict?' Tilda asked tentatively. 'Can you stand up?'

'Stand?' Benedict said. 'Of course I can stand.' He stood. 'I'm not the one divorced from reality! Cursed? Aunt Tilda, I think you need some rest. You're overtired. Overworked. Perhaps you need a break near the sea? I can take over here for a while? Give you time to recuperate?'

Tilda seemed to shrink like a crisp packet in the oven. 'Maybe you're right,' she said softly.

'No!' Minnie said suddenly. 'Give us a chance to find out what's happening. Don't leave.'

'Well,' Tilda replied. 'I'll leave with Benedict now. And I'll think about it. But he may be right.'

Benedict took his aunt's arm firmly. The initial shock appeared to have given way to a determination to make her see sense – his sense. 'Come on,' he told her, 'let's get you home. You need to rest. Don't worry, I'll come back to lock up. You can rely on me, Aunt Tilda.'

He steered her out of the shop without a backwards glance.

'I don't think I like him,' Minnie said.

'Who, Benedict?' Piotr replied.

'Yes. There's something a bit creepy about him, don't you think? He's just the sort of person to send a mummified cat to scare his aunt. Like a practical joke that went way too far.'

'I don't know if he has much of a sense of humour,' Piotr replied.

'And if there's anything we've learned over all of our investigations, it's that you can't judge people by appearances. The baddies don't wear stripy prison tops and black masks on their faces,' Flora said warmly.

Andrew walked over to the shelf, Benedict and Tilda forgotten, for now. Could he hear the cat? He strained his ears, trying to block out the chatter from the others. But there was nothing. No ghostly moans, or spooky meows.

'How should we do this?' he asked. 'Elspeth was a bit vague.'

Sylvie smirked. 'Well, luckily, I'm not vague. I went online before dinner.' She pulled out her phone. 'I've got an app.'

'An app?' Minnie said. 'Are you serious?'

Sylvie held her phone up. There was a pixelated ghost on screen, like something from an ancient video game. 'It detects fields of electromagnetic activity and pinpoints the disturbance within a range of two metres. If there's a mystical moggie in this room, this app will find it.'

'Sylvie, you're brilliant,' Andrew said.

'I know.' She grinned.

'We're going to need snacks too, to keep our strength up during "stakeout",' Flora said. She made air quotes around the word, and Andrew had the feeling that she wasn't taking this very seriously. As she emptied her backpack, he realised she was thinking more sleep-over than seance. 'I brought flapjacks and crisps. And nuts and dried fruit for Sylvie. And some juice. And a rug.'

'Well,' Piotr said, 'we might as well be comfortable.'

Were any of them taking this seriously?

They made a den under an old oak table. It was prob-ably oak, anyway, and definitely old. Flora said it was a refectory table. Andrew took her word for it. There was plenty of room for all of them. Flora lay down her rug and arranged the food, like a picnic.

Andrew lifted the black case from the shelf and laid it on the tabletop. Would they see a ghostly cat? Stretching its leathery sinews and padding its way along the wood? He gulped and rested the palm of his hand on a cabinet. It felt cool, and the crystal goblets inside glistened like watching eyes. He dived under the table to join the others.

Everyone else sat cross-legged, waiting to see what

would happen. The shop was shrouded in darkness. Shadows elongated, swallowing up more and more of the floor, eating chunks of furniture, nibbling at ornaments.

Andrew was listening for the rasping voice of the cat. What if it spoke Ancient Egyptian?

Sylvie had her phone in front of her, watching the screen.

Flora's phone too was set to record any sound they might hear.

Minnie's phone wasn't as good as the twins', so she was using hers to play solitaire.

Piotr chewed flapjacks – they'd decided the crisps were too noisy.

The brown table legs became black. The sharp edges of the cupboards and chairs blended into something more opaque. Crouched shapes in silent wait. The gang too grew quiet. The clicking of Minnie's phone keys stopped. Andrew could see the flash of teeth as Sylvie gave in to nervous laughter. Minnie nudged her still. The gang were shapes too now, dark circles with odd angles as knees and elbows flexed.

'Should we try to speak to it, do you think? If it doesn't speak to us first?' Andrew whispered.

He could feel the others around him breathing. Their

faces were only partly lit from below by the cold light of the screens. They looked like figures from the underworld themselves.

'No,' Piotr replied. 'Elspeth didn't say anything about that, she said to listen.'

'Hush!' Sylvie said. She raised the palm of her hand in their direction.

'Don't talk to him like –' Minnie began.

'Hush! Something's happening,' Sylvie said urgently.

She pointed to her phone. The screen flickered, a thin green line, indicating electromagnetic disturbance, ran across the background in waves. The waves, like a skipping rope speeding up, jumped higher and higher.

Andrew could feel it now.

A wailing, keening noise, right at the very edge of his hearing.

The hairs on the back of his neck bristled. He felt Minnie lean in closer. 'Can you hear that?' she whispered.

He nodded, hard.

He could. A sound like nothing he'd heard before. His hands flew to his ears. The others, too, clamped their hands up, trying to block out the wail.

The green line on Sylvie's phone whipped up and down, faster and faster in a blur of motion.

66

Clawed hands crawled up Andrew's spine. His flesh shivered.

Crash! Something shattered above them. Then again, like ice snapping. Then again. And again. Glass? Was it glass?

Minnie's hands grabbed his arm. He could see terror in the whites of her eyes. Then, her grip lessened. He saw her mouth something.

He lowered his hands. 'What?'

'It's stopped,' she said.

She was right.

The noise had stopped. The shop felt musty and dusty and old, but not full of menace any more.

Had the cat gone?

Andrew crawled out quickly.

He wasn't alone. All the others clambered out behind him, hands mashing ankles, feet treading on fingers. With a few 'ouches' and 'heys' they were all standing in the shop.

What had happened?

Andrew looked at the tabletop. The black case was still there, the clasps closed. But …

The cabinet, which had once held rows of shining goblets, was now full of smashed glass. Every single goblet was shattered and broken. Curls of glass, shards of crystal, were jumbled inside like the ice at the bottom of a cinema cola.

Everything in the cupboard was ruined.

'What. On. Earth?' Flora whispered.

Andrew spun around, looking into all the nooks and crannies and crevices of the shop. Could there be someone hiding? Someone who managed to slip by them, totally unseen and unheard, who managed to open a locked cupboard and smash everything inside without them seeing a single thing.

The shop appeared to be empty. Apart from the gang, who stood with mouths open, or eyes wide, or trembling slightly. Andrew didn't want to be the only one trembling slightly, so he bounced up and down a few times to get himself under control.

Flora and Piotr approached the cabinet. She reached for the handle, turned it, but nothing happened. 'It's locked,' she whispered in awe.

'I don't like this!' Sylvie said. 'It's worse than single magpies or standing on cracks or anything like that! This is violent. We should call Jimmy.'

Jimmy was their special constable friend. Though he had recently been promoted and was a police constable now. He'd helped them out more than once when their cases had become too hot to handle alone.

'Do the police investigate curses?' Minnie said doubtfully.

'Well, this may or may not be a curse,' Flora said, 'but it's definitely criminal damage. He would look into that.'

Andrew moved closer to the cabinet. The vase on top was fine. The candlesticks of burnished silver were still upright. But the crystal was totally ruined.

Street lights flickered on outside, casting an orange glow into the shop.

'You can't say there's no curse now,' he said softly to Flora.

'Someone could have sneaked in and done this!' she said.

'A person no one saw? Or heard opening the cabinet?' Andrew said scornfully. 'What we're dealing with here is some top-dollar, A-star, bona fide paranormal activity. Flora, we don't need a police officer, we need a priest!'

Chapter Nine

Piotr eased Andrew aside and leaned closer, to look at the shattered glass.

'Don't touch anything,' Flora warned, 'Tilda will want Jimmy to take a look; we shouldn't disturb evidence.'

'I won't,' Piotr replied.

They all eyed the cabinet in an eerie silence, each of them with thoughts tumbling through their minds: Was the cat cursed? What did it want? If it wasn't cursed, why did the goblets shatter? What was behind all this?

The bell above the door sounded. Andrew nearly jumped out of his skin.

'What have you done?' The strained, squeaky voice belonged to Benedict. 'What have you done? I knew Aunt Tilda shouldn't have left you here!'

He paced towards the cabinet, face lined with fury.

Andrew turned, his arms out as though he were

trying to hide the damage. 'We didn't do this, the curse did!'

'Curse!' Benedict yelled. 'Curse! You lot are nothing but trouble. You put ideas into the head of an old lady, you run rampage, smashing up the place, and expect me to believe some hocus-pocus? Well, I won't have it. I won't. All of you, out. Now!'

Flora bundled her rug from under the table and held it close. 'You can't really think we'd do this?' she said.

'Well, who else was here?' Benedict said. He reached for the cabinet doors and turned the handle. The cabinet didn't open. 'Locked?' he muttered. There was a tiny key in one of the doors; he twisted it until it clicked. As he opened the doors, small shards of glass fell on to the drawer top. He pushed the door closed quickly. 'I will be finding out exactly the value of the contents of this cabinet and I will be sending you the bill,' he said with a frosty finality. 'Now, out, out!'

There was nothing for it but to leave. Benedict rushed them out on to the street and locked the door firmly behind them.

They were shut out of the shop and shut out of the case.

'We can come back in the morning,' Piotr said. 'We can explain to Tilda what happened. She'll believe us.'

'How can we explain when we don't know what happened?' Sylvie said. 'That whole thing gave me the creeps. I don't know if I even want to go back.'

Marsh Road was properly dark now. Low clouds raced across the night sky as though chased by hounds. Inky darkness seeped between the puddles of street lights. Andrew was glad that he had Piotr to walk home with.

They said goodbye to the girls and set off towards the flats. With each step he felt the tug towards Mum grow stronger. He'd been out for two hours. And the curse had struck. Was she OK? He picked up the pace. Piotr was taller, but he had to take big strides to keep up.

'What should we do next, do you think?' Piotr asked.

'What?'

'We've come to a bit of a dead end, with clues, I mean. We could try Elspeth again, I suppose?'

Andrew didn't reply. Above their heads early buds on tree branches looked like gnarled fingers against the dark sky. He shivered and rucked the collar of his coat up over his ears.

Piotr elbowed him lightly. 'We'll be home soon, don't worry.'

That was the good thing about Piotr. He didn't make a big deal of anything, but he knew when there was something wrong. Andrew smiled gratefully. Piotr was also pretty good at saying the right thing. He didn't just let whatever he was thinking fly straight out of his mouth. Piotr took his time. He only spoke once he'd examined the words from every angle and decided that each one was the right one to use.

Andrew could probably learn something from Piotr. If he could manage to focus for long enough. Which he was pretty sure was impossible. There was a tree that looked exactly like a dinosaur eating a witch. He was about to point it out to Piotr, when Piotr spoke.

'There might be a curse. I'm not saying there isn't. But if there is, then you have to wonder what we can do about it. I mean, it's a *curse*! We can hardly chase it and catch it, can we?' Andrew could see the corner of Piotr's mouth curl into a grin in the glow of the amber street lights. 'But,' Piotr continued, 'if Flora is right, and there isn't a curse, then it must be a person who broke the glasses. And we can catch a person. You see?'

'But there was no one in the shop but us,' Andrew said. 'I still think we need a priest.'

* * *

'Mum?' Andrew turned the key and stepped into the hallway of the flat.

'In here, sweetheart.' Mum's voice came from the living room.

'How are you feeling?' Andrew called, pulling off his jacket and stretching to reach a peg. He wandered into the living room.

Mum was sitting in her armchair. There was a cup of tea steaming on the coffee table in front of her, alongside a packet of biscuits. 'I'm just having a snack,' she said.

'Oh, sorry,' he said, dropping on to the sofa.

'Why are you sorry?'

'Because I wasn't here to get it for you.'

'I can open biscuits, you know!'

'I know.'

Andrew helped himself to one.

'So, what have you been up to?' Mum asked. 'You were with Piotr?'

Andrew chewed, working the sweet mush off his teeth with his tongue. He didn't want to worry Mum. But at the same time, a cabinet of crystal goblets had practically exploded all over them because of an angry Egyptian cat. Worry, explosion, worry, explosion. He paused, trying to do what Piotr did before he spoke.

74

It was no use.

He swallowed. 'We were ghost hunting! Well, sort of. We listened to the voice of the cat and it rained down destruction and chaos on Marsh Road.'

'What?'

'It was like an explosion. Crystals flying everywhere. I was lucky not to get decapitated.'

'Andrew!'

He'd gone too far.

'Oh, well, no, not really. But it was really dramatic. You should have seen it. Will you come tomorrow to the shop? I can show you.'

Mum pressed her lips together until they looked white. Then she said, 'Maybe not tomorrow. Maybe the next day.'

Andrew took another bite of his biscuit. Chewed. Swallowed. Something wasn't right here. It wasn't just that she was worried about him. He had a twitchy feeling as he watched Mum sip her tea.

'Did you sleep all right last night?' he asked suspiciously.

'Oh, Andrew. It's fine, honestly.'

'Did you have another bad dream?'

'I don't want to talk about it.'

75

'So you did then?'

Mum put down her cup. Was her hand shaking? 'I'm sure it's nothing. I'm probably just overtired by going out and starting work again. It will probably just take a little bit of time for things to settle down.'

But Mum had hardly been at work. She'd only been there an hour or two, tops! Andrew felt a twisting worm of worry inside. 'What are you dreaming?'

'I said you don't need to worry about it, it's nothing.'

'Mum, please.'

She sighed. 'I don't know, sweetheart. And I don't mean that I don't want to tell you. I mean that I really don't know. I can smell the smoke from the fire in my dream. And hear it too. And it feels like someone is watching me, but not helping.'

'Who?'

'No one. It's just a dream. I was on my own that night. I'm probably just eating cheese too close to bedtime. Forget I said anything, OK?'

Andrew had no intention of forgetting about Mum's problems. But he had no idea what he could do about them. It felt as though the curse was creeping along the dark shadows of Marsh Road towards them.

Chapter Ten

'Benedict was so cross, he might not let us back in,' Minnie said.

They were huddled the following morning behind the fruit and veg stall. The air smelled of citrus and tomatoes, flowers and potatoes. The trader yelled about his bargain onions while the gang spoke in hushed whispers.

'Tilda will let us in,' Andrew said confidently. 'She wants the curse lifted.'

'Let's assume,' Flora said, 'that the crystal goblets didn't smash because of the workings of some mysterious force. Let's assume that a person is responsible.'

Andrew bristled. A cabinet of crystals spontaneously combusted! There was no one around, except for them. Flora wouldn't recognise a curse if it dropped ectoplasm sandwiches on her head.

She noticed his eye roll.

'Let's just assume, for a minute, that's all,' she said. 'If there isn't a curse, then something made those glasses break. What might it have been?'

'We looked last night,' Piotr said. 'There was nothing there. Just broken glasses and old dust. The cabinet was locked. We've no explanation for why they all smashed at the same time.'

'You think it's a curse too?' Sylvie asked.

Piotr's cheeks blushed pink. 'I don't think it's not a curse. That's not the same thing.'

Minnie, who had been quiet up until that point, spoke. 'You've got to admit, Flora, it's all looking a bit cursey right now.'

'No, it isn't. We just didn't find a better explanation. But we will. We should take another look. Maybe it was because we were so jumpy last night, and it was dark; maybe we missed something. A clue?'

Andrew peered around the plastic awning at the edge of the stall. He had a clear view of Meeke and Sons from where he stood. The shop was open, with the shutters up. He could see Tilda inside, wrapping a vase for a customer. There was no sign of Benedict. Andrew waited until the customer left the shop, cradling his purchase, before he said to the others, 'I think we should go for it.'

He led the way, jangling the bell as he walked in. 'Hello?' he said. He could see straight away that the cabinet had been cleared of debris. The shelves were swept of fragments. The candlesticks were inside now.

As they walked in, Tilda called out a tremulous welcome. 'Andrew! Oh, and Minnie! And everyone!'

'Hi, Tilda,' Piotr said. 'Is it all right if we come in?'

'Of course it's all right. Are you OK? Benedict told me about last night. It sounds horrible. Just horrible. What a thing to happen. You know, when I saw the Eye of Ra, I was terrified that I might have imagined it. But now this, it's even worse! None of you were hurt?'

'We're fine,' Flora said. They joined Tilda near the counter. She looked tired, Andrew thought. Her eyes were red-rimmed.

'We didn't do it, you know,' Minnie said, 'we didn't smash the glasses.'

'Of course not,' Tilda replied. 'Oh, you mustn't mind Benedict. He's very protective. He cleared up so that I wouldn't cut myself on the glass. So thoughtful. He's going to try to be here much more often, he says. He's coming in later this morning. Every cloud has a silver lining.'

'Tilda,' Flora said. 'Did you watch him clean the

79

cabinet? Did you notice anything? Anything that might explain the smashed crystal?'

'There was nothing, dear,' Tilda said. 'Once the smashed goblets were cleared it was just empty shelves.'

Piotr frowned. 'And you didn't discuss calling the police, at all?'

Tilda raised her palms. 'What on earth would I say to them?'

'The cat wouldn't leave a trace for them to find,' Andrew said. 'What we need is to shower the place with holy water.'

'Let's just consider some less wet solutions first?' Flora said. She peered at the front of the cupboard, at its shelves, at the base and the legs and the occasional tables on either side, looking at them from every angle. 'There's nothing unusual,' she said finally. 'We need to think about opportunity. Who's been near the cabinet in the time between the cat being delivered on Monday morning and Tuesday night when the glasses broke?' She looked at Tilda for an answer.

'Well, er, me, and all of you. And Andrew's mum, of course, for a little bit. Benedict, I suppose. And the customers.'

Flora's face fell. 'That's a lot of people.'

Tilda flushed pink. 'Well, not really. I didn't open at all on Tuesday morning. And Mondays are usually a bit slow.'

'How many customers did you have?' Piotr asked.

'Two,' Tilda whispered.

'Two?' Sylvie gasped.

'They both seemed like such nice people. I can't imagine they would know anything about what's been going on here.'

'The alternative is that we suspect a thousand-year-old dead cat,' Flora said firmly.

Andrew glanced at the black case which had been put back on the shelf. He still thought the cat did it, no matter what Flora said. All you had to do was look at it to know something wasn't right. It was sinister, suspicious, and other 's' noises. He would go along with Flora, for now. But at the first sign of a phantom manifestation, he was looking up the pope's phone number.

He was brought back to the room by the sight of Flora reaching for her notebook. 'Can you describe the customers? Do you remember?'

Tilda nodded slowly. 'There was a nice young man who bought a nineteenth-century ewer.'

'A lady sheep?' Andrew asked.

'No, that's a ewe. A ewer is a jug for holding water.'

'Oh.'

Flora tried to squish her smile. 'Do you know his name?'

Tilda shook her head. 'No, but he said it would look nice in his bed and breakfast. I think he said it was near the stage school.'

'He should be easy to find,' Piotr said confidently.

'There was a woman too, looking for an antique sofa. I didn't have anything suitable, but she left her name and number in case I find anything she might like soon. I have it here somewhere.' Tilda rifled around in the piles of rubbish on her desk until she came across a slim white card. 'Aha! This is it.'

She handed it to Piotr.

Andrew peered over his shoulder. The card had an elegant scrawled font, pretending to be handwriting. It read 'The Hon. Miranda Fairbanks, Old Wynd House, Old Wynd'. It was as fancy as sparkly pants.

'Anyone else?' Minnie asked.

Tilda scrunched her shoulders. 'That's it.'

'At least that makes our job easy,' Flora said brightly.

'What job?' Andrew asked.

'Interviewing the witnesses.'

Chapter Eleven

'We've got two people to interview,' Piotr said.

'Three,' Flora replied.

'Three? Tilda only had two customers.'

'Benedict,' Flora said. 'He was in the shop between the mummy arriving and the goblets shattering. And he was the one who cleared up the broken pieces. We have to talk to him.'

They were outside Meeke's. The spring sun was higher and it was bright enough for a few people to even be wearing sunglasses. In the sunlight, it was strange to remember how scared they'd been the night before. And how angry Benedict had been.

'Well,' Piotr said, 'if we've got three witnesses to interview, we should split up. We'll get it done quicker if we do.'

Andrew looked at the gilt card that Tilda had given them. 'Bagsy the Hon. Miranda Fairbanks,' he said.

'Me too! She sounds nice,' Sylvie said.

'She sounds rich,' Minnie muttered.

'I think Benedict needs to be handled carefully,' Piotr said. 'I'll take him.'

'That leaves me and Flora to find the bed and breakfast owner,' Minnie said.

'Good,' Flora said. 'Remember, everyone, we want to find out whether anyone saw anything suspicious near the cabinet, and we also want to find out whether Tilda has any enemies, anyone who would want to frighten her.'

'Anyone who'd want to lay a curse on her,' Andrew corrected.

'Any enemies at all,' Piotr said softly.

Flora and Minnie headed off together towards the theatre. Some of the trees in the theatre square were in blossom, wads of candyfloss colour that smelled of soap and spring-time. Individual petals blew from the trees, banking in summer drifts along the path. Flora felt herself smiling, despite the memory of the smashed crystal in the shadows.

There was no such thing as a curse.

The bright sunlight speckling the path made the very idea seem ridiculous.

But she had no explanation for the smashed crystal.

She had no explanation for the smashed crystal – *yet*, she corrected.

Minnie was looking at her phone, tapping the screen. 'There's a bed and breakfast just on the other side of the theatre,' she said. 'It's called the Curtain Call.'

'Let's check it out.'

The building itself looked like most of the town houses in the area, three storeys with a flat front, like playing cards laid for a game of solitaire. But the sign above the steps read 'Curtain Call B&B, en suite rooms, cable TVs'. A tragedy and comedy mask hung on either side of the sign – one face grinning maniacally, the other frowning like an annoyed head teacher.

Minnie led the way up the steps and rapped on the front door.

Flora noticed that the steps had been swept and the door knocker was brightly polished.

The door was opened by a man with night-black hair that rose in improbable curls all around his head. His suit was pinstriped and pin-sharp. He smiled widely. 'Can I help you?' he said.

'I'm Minnie, this is Flora. We were hoping we might talk to you about the junk shop on Marsh Road? Meeke and Sons? There have been some strange things happening and we're looking for witnesses.'

'The junk shop?' the man's brows creased as he thought.

'Yes. Were you there on Monday?' Minnie asked.

His brow cleared. 'Oh, of course. It had slipped my mind, but that's where I got the lovely new toilette set. Well, not *new*, I think it must be quite old actually. But new to me and new to the Hamlet Suite. Come in, come in.'

He stepped aside and let them into the hallway.

Flora gasped. The decor was more overwhelming than a Japanese pop video. Every single surface and wall had something adorning it. Playbills, posters and programmes had been framed and the faces of stars paraded across the hall. A Welsh dresser stood on the tiled floor, each shelf dotted with theatre memorabilia, signed photos and tickets. Beyond the hall stacks and stacks of books filled dark wood shelves. Flora glanced at their spines as they walked further into the house – plays, poetry, classic literature. They smelled of dust and – Flora knew this from a more disgusting article in *New Scientist* – the waft of paper-mite poop.

It was, weirdly, quite a nice smell. For poop.

86

Andrew would be gutted not to see this.

They stopped in a back kitchen. Again, every surface gleamed, but it was still homely, with lots of wooden cabinets and a cat curled up on a comfy chair. It had found a patch of weak sunlight and it wasn't shifting for anyone. It opened a lazy eye as they walked in.

'Ignore Romeo,' the man said. 'He sleeps for eighteen hours a day.' He waved towards the kitchen table. 'Sit,' he said, 'and tell me what's going on.'

They dropped on to a bench. The table had been scrubbed and smelled faintly of lemon detergent. Or maybe it was the smell of the citrus fruit in a bowl in the middle of the table. It was definitely a nice place to stay, Flora thought. A fan of interesting-looking magazines lay at the end of the table: home decorating, photography, architecture. Beautiful images of rainforests and rooftops. Her fingers itched to pick up one with a picture of a glass bridge on the front. Surely a glass bridge was a terrible idea; its structural weakness made it a death trap?

She was brought back to the moment by the man sitting down across from them. 'Your bums are sitting where some very famous actors have perched, you know,' he said with a grin. 'Olivier, Day-Lewis, Richard

Harris, they all sat where you are now, over the years.'

Flora wasn't sure exactly who all those people were, but it was nice to share bum space with probably-famous actors.

'What's your name?' Minnie asked.

'Winston. Winston Fropp. I've run the Curtain Call for the last forty years. I know, I don't look old enough! But it was my mother's before me, so I've been here since I was a nipper.'

'It's nice,' Flora said.

'It is. But you didn't come to talk to me about well-run bed and breakfasts, did you?'

Flora smiled shyly. Winston was as overwhelming as his decor.

'There was a delivery of a strange object at Meeke's, and ever since then some very peculiar things have been happening. A weird vision, and a cupboard full of crystal goblets smashed all by themselves. That happened the evening after your visit.'

'Well, it had nothing to do with me!' Winston said.

'No, no, we're just asking you whether you saw anything strange while you were in the shop? Anything suspicious?'

Winston sat down; the bench creaked in protest. 'That shop is full of the strangest, weirdest things imaginable. It all looks suspicious!'

'Fair point,' Minnie said.

'Was there anyone in the shop with you? Or maybe you saw someone nearby, or, well, anything?' Flora tried again.

Winston shook his head. 'I'm sorry. I'd help if I could, but it was all just as it always is. Lots of old things all piled in a heap. The lady who runs it was there, of course, but the shop was very quiet. I'm surprised she manages to stay open. I liked the jug, but I bought it mostly because I felt sorry for her. Would you like to see it?'

Flora glanced at Minnie, then shook her head. 'I'm sure it's great, but I don't think it's a clue. Can you think of any reason why someone would want to scare Tilda?'

'I'm sure it's just a prank,' Winston said. 'Actors do that sort of thing to each other all the time. Though smashing crystal seems a bit far to go for a joke.'

'Maybe you're right,' Flora said, thinking that there was no way he was right.

'Well, let me know if there's anything more I can do for you.' Winston pushed himself up from the table. It was clear he had nothing useful to add, so Flora followed, with Minnie right behind.

They went back through the cool corridor.

Just as Winston placed his hand on the door lock to let them out, he paused. 'Why are you two interested anyway?' he asked.

'We investigate mysteries,' Flora said simply.

'Ooh, Little Miss Marples! How exciting,' Winston said. 'This area really is coming up in the world! New flats, a health food deli and now junior detectives. Marsh Road is the place to be these days.' He opened the door. 'Do call again if I can help. And good luck with your investigations!'

With that, the two were back on the street.

'Well, nice, but useless,' Flora said. 'I hope Piotr, Andrew and Sylvie are having more luck!'

Chapter Twelve

Piotr thought it would be a good idea to ambush Benedict. To interview him before he went into the shop and was on home ground. That way he might be caught by surprise. He might even give something away.

So, Piotr waited at the end of Marsh Road, far enough away from Meeke's to not catch Tilda's eye, but close enough that he'd be able to spot Benedict. He found a patch of sunlight warming a wall, so settled against the bricks to wait.

It didn't take long.

He soon spotted Benedict striding through the pedestrian zone. He looked smarter today, his suit pressed and his hair brushed. He was smiling at the world in general and the shoppers on Marsh Road in particular. As he got closer, Piotr could hear Benedict greeting strangers like long-lost friends.

'Good morning, madam, perhaps we'll see you in Meeke and Sons today? Sir, hello! It's an excellent day to peruse quality antiques!' Most shoppers, clutching their bags of potatoes and lettuces and apples, looked confused.

Well, at least Benedict was feeling talkative.

Piotr sauntered towards Benedict, casually. 'Morning!' he said brightly.

Benedict gave a wide grin, before recognition wiped it from his face. 'Oh,' he said, 'it's you.'

'Yes, Piotr. We met yesterday. I just wanted to say sorry about last night. I promise we had nothing to do with the damage.'

Benedict gave a humourless laugh. 'I suppose the fairies did it? Oh no, I was forgetting, it was the curse.' He waggled his fingers as he said the word 'curse' – a witch casting a spell.

'Tilda thinks so. We're not so sure.' It didn't seem to be the time to mention Andrew. 'Did you see anything or anyone suspicious in the shop at all? Anything that might explain how the crystal shattered?'

'Why, yes, I did, as a matter of fact.' Benedict leaned in conspiratorially. 'I saw five children who were standing right next to the cabinet all looking very guilty. That's what I saw.'

Piotr felt his pulse quicken, a warmth of anger spread through his chest. 'I said we didn't do it and I meant it. We're trying to help your aunt. Which is more than you're doing.' He spoke loudly, forcefully. Shoppers stopped to watch.

Benedict pulled himself up to his full height and glared at Piotr. 'How dare you! I would do anything for Tilda. That's why I'm here. The poor thing is under a lot of stress. She hasn't got a business brain and the shop isn't busy. It's no wonder she's started imagining things, and you lot are making it worse. The sooner she hands the shop over to me and my investors and goes for a long, well-deserved rest, the better!'

Piotr took a few deep breaths. His brain was whizzing. Benedict wanted to take over the shop. He wanted Tilda out of the picture. He had a motive. 'Will Tilda let you take over?' Piotr asked. 'She loves that shop.'

Benedict pressed his palms together and smiled a smarmy sort of smile. 'Not only will she let me, she's already talked about packing her bags. She might even be gone by the weekend. We're looking at brochures for hotels by the sea this afternoon.'

Piotr watched in stunned silence as Benedict gave a tight little bow and headed towards Meeke's.

Someone was trying to frighten Tilda out of her own shop.

And he had a strong suspicion that that person was her own nephew.

Chapter Thirteen

Andrew stood, beside Sylvie, in front of one of the most elegant houses he had ever seen. Like an understated wedding cake, it was white, tiered, and oozed charm. Old Wynd was a mews style backstreet, old stables that had been converted into very neat little houses. There were window boxes stuffed full of early primroses and mini daffodils.

Three stone steps led up to a black front door. A lion's head gripped a round knocker in its teeth, like a baby's teething ring, Andrew thought.

'Wow,' he said. 'It's like something from a magazine.'

Sylvie shrugged. 'It's all right, I suppose.'

Andrew squished a smirk. Sylvie was trying to be cool, but he knew she was as impressed as he was. If Sylvie had been visiting the queen, she'd pretend it was an everyday occurrence.

With her nose held firmly in the air, Sylvie marched up to the door, lifted the heavy knocker and gave the door two sharp raps.

A flurry of excited barking rushed towards them from inside the house. And was halted abruptly as a dog thunked into the door. The jolt only silenced it for a second though. Then it was off again in a fury of yaps: 'Grrr, yarrr, yowwwww!'

'Get back, Bruiser!' a voice said. Then there were sounds of shuffling and more yapping before the door opened.

Immediately a white ball of fluff launched itself down the steps.

'Bruiser!'

But the woman was completely ignored by the little dog. His yaps and howls turned to whimpers of joy as he sniffed and licked the new arrivals. Sylvie reached down to pat him and he instantly threw himself on to his back – awkward considering the steps – and kicked his legs in the air.

'He wants his tummy rubbed,' Andrew said.

'He wants his head examined,' the woman said. 'He's meant to be a guard dog, but apart from the manic barking, he's useless at it.'

She bent down and scooped up Bruiser, who wiggled and wriggled in her arms.

Now that the dog was more or less under control, Andrew was able to look at the woman. She was young-looking, and her dark hair was styled into loose curls. Her clothes were all shades of beige wool, everything from dark tan to latte. She was more stylish than anyone Andrew had seen in a very long time.

'How can I help?' the woman asked. 'You two look too young to be selling anything.'

'Ms Fairbanks? We were hoping to be able to talk to you about the Meeke and Sons junk shop,' Sylvie said in her most polite voice.

'Call me Miranda, do. Come in. I'm afraid you'll have to excuse the mess.'

Andrew wondered what on earth Miranda was talking about. The hall gleamed; its warm wooden floors and stair-case were polished. Light seemed to bounce around the space, making it feel like a summer day, rather than early spring. It was one of the nicest houses he'd ever been inside.

'So, I'm negotiating the price of a sofa with children, am I?' Miranda said. 'Are you good hagglers? Wheeler-dealers? I should warn you, I'm a pretty good bargain hunter myself.'

What was she talking about?

Then Andrew remembered: Miranda had left her card with Tilda in case Tilda found the perfect antique sofa for her to buy. She'd assumed they'd come with news of that. It was a good way to get her to talk, but it wouldn't take long before she realised that there was no sofa.

'It's going to go here, in the new extension,' Miranda said, leading them into a beautiful big kitchen. A wall of glass doors looked out on to the garden; acid lime leaves splattered the dark trees like graffiti. The space inside the doors was empty and echoey – waiting for a comfy sofa. 'Has Tilda found something suitable?'

There wasn't anywhere to sit, so Andrew leaned against a new kitchen cabinet – it still had stickers from the shop on it.

'Tilda's still looking,' Sylvie said firmly. 'But she asked us to talk to you for her, to find out if there's anything useful you might add to what she knows already.'

Nice! Sylvie wasn't lying at all! She was just introducing a new subject, without mentioning it to Miranda. Smooth as whipped cream.

'You went in to Meeke's on Monday,' Andrew said, 'to see whether she had anything suitable?'

'That's right.'

'Did you take a look around the shop?'

'Of course. I must have been there for about an hour. She had a Welsh dresser that might have been good just there –' she gestured to an empty wall '– but, in the end, I decided not to buy it. At least not until I have the right sofa. The lady in the shop tried very hard to sell it to me though. I was impressed by her chutzpah.'

'Did you notice a cabinet, full of crystal goblets?' Sylvie asked.

Andrew watched Miranda's face, alert for any flicker of guilt. But her expression didn't change one iota. Either she knew nothing, or the Botox was still fresh.

'Are you trying to sell me that nasty cabinet?' Miranda said. 'It was a horrible 1990s reproduction, in my opinion. Nothing antique about it at all. I didn't give it a second glance.'

'You know a lot about antiques?' Sylvie said.

'Of course! I'm an archaeologist!'

Andrew felt a sudden shiver of excitement. An archaeologist? 'Do you know a lot about Egypt and mummies and things?'

Miranda wrinkled her nose. 'That's all anyone thinks about when they hear the word archaeology. That or Indiana Jones. No, that isn't my thing at all. I specialise in

Northern Europe, post-Roman Britain and the early medieval period. I couldn't care less about pharaohs and all that.'

Oh.

'Not like my grandfather,' Miranda added.

Oh?

'He was obsessed with Egypt. Spent all his days filching things in the sand for museums back in Britain. Got him a knighthood in the end.'

'Your grandfather collected mummies?' Sylvie whispered.

'Yes.' Miranda sniffed. 'Nasty things. Give me a nice stained-glass window over that any day.'

'Where are your grandfather's collections now?' Andrew asked breathlessly.

'All over the place. Museums in Oxford, London, Edinburgh. A few private collections. I've even got some of his more tatty stuff in the loft here!'

Here? In this house?

Andrew almost yelped with excitement. Bruiser must have sensed it, because he gave a loud bark, making them all jump.

'Bruiser!' Miranda said. 'What's wrong?' Bruiser clattered around the kitchen, paws and claws scraping the new tiles. 'Bruiser! Stop it! Sorry about the dog. He's given to these mad moments. He's upset by new people. It took him months to get used to my new boyfriend. But you like Benny now, don't you, Bruiser?'

The dog did another overenthusiastic lap of the kitchen, then flopped into a fluffy pink bed.

'Right. So, have you got everything you need to find me a sofa?' Miranda asked.

'For now,' Andrew said. 'For now.'

Chapter Fourteen

'So, an Egyptologist was in Tilda's shop on Monday?' Minnie said in wonder.

They were all in Eileen's cafe, in their favourite spot by the window. Andrew and Sylvie had told the others about their visit to the Hon. Miranda.

Andrew nodded his head vigorously. 'I know! That's suspicious, isn't it?'

'Technically,' Sylvie said pointedly, 'she isn't an Egyptologist, she's a medievalist. But she definitely had the opportunity to send a mummy to Tilda.'

'But motive, though?' Flora asked. 'What would be her motive?' She tapped a pencil against her notepad, leaving dead-fly dots on the paper.

'Why would *anyone* want to put a curse on poor Tilda?' Andrew said. It seemed so unlikely.

'Even a fake curse,' Flora added.

Piotr tapped the table with his fingertips. 'I haven't told you about Benedict yet,' he said.

Flora held her pencil, ready to take notes.

'Benedict said that he wants to take charge of the shop, to try to make it profitable. He's going to talk to Tilda today about places she can go while he and his pals run the place.'

A stunned silence settled over the table as everyone thought about what that might mean.

'He's been saying that it's all in her imagination, and that we've been making things worse,' Minnie said softly.

'Maybe he sent the mummy to frighten Tilda in the first place, then he tries to convince her that it's all in her head,' Flora added, scribbling quickly across her notebook. 'Then he somehow made the goblets break. I don't know how yet, maybe with a tripwire or mini firework or something.'

'We didn't see anything in the cabinet like that,' Piotr objected. 'Nor did Tilda.'

'Yes, but Benedict was the one who cleared up the mess. He might have removed the evidence before we had a proper chance to look.'

Andrew felt a flash of anger. Who could be mean enough to hurt Mum, or Tilda for that matter? They were both lovely. Mum especially. He wondered whether she had left the flat at all today. He hoped so. But she was scared right now. Just like Tilda. And it was Tilda's own nephew who had made her feel that way. Either faked a curse, like Flora thought, or he'd really cursed her. He wasn't sure which was worse. 'What a mean, low-life, good-for-nothing –'

'Yes,' Flora interrupted, before Andrew had really got going. 'Yes, he might be. But did Benedict have the opportunity? He arrived at Tilda's shop yesterday at the same time as me and Sylvie. We were there the whole time and I didn't see him go near the cabinet. Did you, Sylvie?'

Sylvie shook her head.

'So –' Flora checked her notebook '– we have Miranda, who has access to ancient artefacts and was in the shop for an hour nosing around, and we have Benedict, who was never alone in the shop, but wants Tilda gone. One suspect with opportunity, but no motive. And another with motive, but no opportunity.'

Piotr nodded slowly. 'We have to consider them both as suspects for now,' he said. 'So what are we going to do about it?'

Andrew chased the tip of his straw with his tongue as it spun inside his can of pop, like a frog trying to catch a fly. Two suspects. Either of them might have put the curse on Tilda. On Mum. He bit the tip of the straw, squishing it flat.

'It seems to me,' Piotr said, 'that we need to concentrate on looking for a motive for Miranda and an opportunity for Benedict. Let's follow Miranda, and see if we can find out more about her. Look her up on the internet too. We need information more than anything. For Benedict, we have to work out exactly what he did when he came to Meeke's on Tuesday evening. Could he have tampered with the cabinet in any way?'

'How will we do that?' Sylvie asked.

'You and Flora were there the whole time. You can do a reconstruction, to see what you remember.'

'So,' Minnie said, 'we split up. Flora and Sylvie go to Meeke's and the rest of us trail Miranda?'

Yes! Excellent! A suspect to follow. Andrew wriggled in his seat.

Then he remembered he hadn't seen Mum since breakfast, and now it was dinner time. Had she eaten? Was she OK? As soon as he'd had the thought it seemed to mushroom into a hundred worries. 'I might have to go home first,' he said, deflating a little.

'That's all right.' Piotr gave him a look that was full of

understanding. 'We shouldn't all go together to spy on Miranda anyway. We need to blend into the background. A big gang of us would look too suspicious. I'll take first watch.'

There was a tiny bit of pop left at the bottom of Andrew's can. He sucked it up with a throaty gurgle which made Sylvie roll her eyes and Minnie laugh. He couldn't really explain why he was so worried about Mum. But making Minnie laugh made him feel that he didn't have to explain. She was still his friend.

It was decided that Piotr and Minnie would take today's watch between them, and see if Miranda did anything peculiar. If that didn't work, then they might have to find a way to snoop a little closer.

But they had a plan, and Andrew could go back to Mum without feeling he was letting down his friends. Much.

Chapter Fifteen

Leaving the others in the cafe was difficult. Andrew couldn't help but wonder what they would find out without him. But Mum, at home, was like a magnet pulling him closer. She was the most important thing, after all. He rushed along Marsh Road. At the flats, he let himself in and listened in the hallway. Was Mum in? Was she resting?

He could hear the low murmur of a radio from the living room. He hung up his coat and dropped his keys into the ceramic holder he'd made in Year Three. The others would be on their stakeouts, or reconstruction, or just generally having fun now. If he was with them, he'd be a spy, in a trench coat, with a trilby hat, standing under rain clouds. Or he'd be a sharp detective, ordering people about at the scene of the crime. Whatever he was, he wouldn't be making sandwiches and worrying about whether Mum was well enough to catch the bus to her outpatient appointments.

Maybe he could still be involved? He never had asked Mum about the delivery driver. He hadn't wanted to upset her. But maybe she was well enough to handle talking about it?

He wandered into the living room. Mum was lying on the sofa, a rug pulled over her legs. She was looking at a battered photo. Andrew recognised it.

He wouldn't be asking Mum about the delivery driver today.

She was holding the only photo she had of Andrew's dad.

'Hi,' he said softly.

'Hello, love.'

'What are you doing with that?'

Mum folded her hands over the image, protecting it. 'Just reminding myself what he looked like, that's all.'

'We don't need him,' Andrew said. 'We don't need anyone.' Andrew didn't think about his dad often. He had never known him. He'd left when Andrew was a tiny baby and he hadn't stayed in touch. But whenever he did think about his dad, Andrew felt a prickly, uncomfortable feeling in his chest. He sat down on the end of the sofa and tucked the rug in place around Mum's knees. 'You've got me,' he said.

Mum smiled. 'I know. I'm very lucky.'

'What have you been up to today?' Andrew asked.

Mum sighed and let the photo drop into her lap. 'Nothing much.'

'Have you been out?'

'No.'

'Have you been out since Monday?' Andrew asked.

'What is this, the Spanish Inquisition?' Mum said with a laugh.

That meant no, she hadn't. 'Do you feel poorly? Does anything hurt?'

Mum shook her head. 'I just haven't got around to it, that's all.'

'Tilda needs you, you know. She's in trouble in the shop.'

'Tilda only took me on as a favour, to help me out. She doesn't need me.' Mum settled back on to the sofa with a sigh. Her eyelids drooped and her lashes looked blonde against the dark patches under her eyes.

Andrew let her rest. It was what she needed most, after all. Having him nagging her, or asking questions, or poking around in her emotions like rooting for a pair of socks in a drawer wasn't going to do her any good.

What she needed was a great big dose of Andrew-fication. 'Your hair is shocking!' he said.

The corner of her mouth twitched, but she didn't open her eyes.

'What you need is an immediate emergency hairbrush and updo.'

Mum giggled.

'Don't move. I'm going to call the fourth emergency service – Hairdresserboy!'

He launched himself up off the sofa and ran into Mum's room. He grabbed a brush and comb from her dresser, a scrunchy, anything he thought might help to make her feel a bit better. He snapped some sparkly clips on to the edge of his jeans pocket. Then, back in the living room, he dropped to his knees behind her head and began to brush her hair. Long even strokes teased out knots and tugged gently at her scalp. He could sense her relaxing. As soon as her blonde hair was clear of tangles, he scooped it into a swirl. It felt dry and brittle, but as he brushed he worked a shine into it.

'And what style would madam like today? At what event will madam be appearing?' he asked.

'The palace has requested my attendance at a ball later tonight,' Mum said in her poshest voice. 'Something to do with a prince and a lost slipper. An odd theme for a party, but what can you expect from royals?'

'So, you require an updo suitable for a princess? No problem.' Andrew looped a long section of hair around the crown of her head and used a diamanté clip to hold it in place. Then he added extra sections, plaiting in lengths as he went. His fingers worked deftly. Over the past year he had done Mum's hair countless times. He had thought those days were over, but if he'd been wrong, well, he could live with it. Eventually Mum wore a circlet of woven gold hair. Andrew added a few more clips to hold it still.

By the time he stood up, Mum was grinning like a princess before a crowd. 'You're an angel,' she said.

'Hairdresserboy saves the day!' he replied.

And while it would have been good to be with the gang, to be out investigating, it was good to see Mum smile. It was his job to make sure she was happy.

Chapter Sixteen

Piotr and Minnie were on the terracotta-coloured sofa in Minnie's living room. Minnie had her dad's laptop open and was busy searching for everything she could find about the Honourable Miranda Fairbanks.

'She gets to call herself Lady!' Minnie said in an awed voice. 'Like something from a Disney movie!'

Piotr shrugged. She could call herself anything she liked; what he wanted to know was, did she have a motive for creating a curse? 'What else is there?'

Minnie scrolled down, clicking on a few interesting-looking articles. 'She teaches history at a college. There are a few pictures of her at university. They're just in old magazine articles about who was at what posh dinner.'

Piotr leaned in to see. The photos showed a girl with dark hair and big eyes standing in a white dress looking uncomfortable. 'She looks too sweet to want to frighten Tilda.'

'Looks can be deceiving, Piotr,' Minnie said sternly. 'But there's nothing that could be a motive here. Wait! There's a link to her grandfather here.' She clicked, and a black-and-white photograph of a man in military uniform appeared on screen. 'Sir Douglas Fairbanks served under Lieutenant-General Montgomery in Egypt during the Second World War,' she read. 'Wow! That's him, in Egypt! He might have gone straight from taking this picture to discovering the mummified cat!'

'He probably had to finish fighting in the war first,' Piotr said. But it was weird to be looking at a photo of the man whose discovery had started all this trouble.

Minnie sighed and closed the laptop. 'There's nothing here,' she said. 'No motive. I think what we need is boots on the ground.'

'Let's go and spy on the Lady!' Piotr said.

Piotr leaned casually against a wall at the corner of Old Wynd Mews and Church Road. From here he could see the front door of Old Wynd House, but was far enough away not to attract attention. He hoped. He let his arms flop down by his sides and tilted his head as though his neck was missing a bone or two. He tried to look like a teenage boy with attitude. Like Lowdog and his mates, who used to hang out on a bench near the market, until the newsagents installed a machine that made a horrible high-pitched sound that only kids and dogs could hear and it irritated Lowdog away.

It was tough to look cool.

It made his back ache.

'What are you doing?' Minnie asked. 'You look like jelly.' She was leaning beside him, hands in her pockets and one foot flat against the bricks. She actually did look cool.

'Nothing,' he said.

He was about to change position and try to look like a sensible young man waiting for a friend, when the door to Old Wynd House opened. A woman stepped out. He recognised her from the photo Minnie had shown him online. Miranda, a few years older but definitely her. A dog trotted beside her, clipped on to a shiny pink lead.

The perfect trailing opportunity.

'She's walking Bruiser,' Minnie said.

He nudged Minnie and they crossed the road quickly. With their backs to Old Wynd Mews, they stopped in front of a shop window, pretending to admire the pottery bowls and jugs on display. But he could see Miranda and her yappy dog clearly reflected in the glass. She set off towards Theatre Square.

Piotr and Minnie followed at a distance, always keeping her in sight but never getting too close. Once or twice she stopped to let Bruiser sniff a lamp post and leave his own wee-mail. When that happened, Piotr bent to tie a shoelace, or Minnie stopped to pat her pockets as though looking for a ringing phone.

Once they reached the square, Miranda unclipped Bruiser's lead and the little dog bounded towards the bins, leaping to try and grab an overhanging chip wrapper.

'Bruiser, no!' he heard Miranda shout, but the dog ignored her, lost in his own world of delicious smells and abandoned fish batter.

Piotr and Minnie slid behind a plane tree and watched.

Miranda wandered over to one of the park benches. The day was a bit cold, but weak afternoon sunshine filtered through the branches. She closed her eyes and turned her face to the light. Her legs crossed at the ankle and she relaxed back against the wooden slats.

She sat like that for a while. 'Do you think she's gone to sleep?' Minnie whispered.

'Hush.'

It was at that moment that Miranda stretched, took out her phone and tapped the screen. She held it to her ear and waited. When the person at the other end picked up, Piotr was just close enough to hear Miranda say a name.

His jaw dropped.

This changed everything.

Chapter Seventeen

Flora and Sylvie's task was to work out whether Benedict had had the opportunity to set up the explosion of glasses in the cabinet. Flora didn't believe that the shop was cursed, which meant there had to be some practical explanation. Was Benedict the smasher?

'Can we do a reconstruction in the shop?' Flora wondered.

'I don't see why not,' Sylvie said. 'Tilda might ask what we're up to. And it might be a bit embarrassing if Benedict is there. But a little bit of embarrassment is no reason not to do something.'

Flora sighed. Actually, she didn't like being embarrassed at all, but Sylvie, who wanted to be an actress, had elephant-hide skin.

They walked to the shop.

Tilda was at her desk at the far end of the room. She

gave them a smile and a wave, but without much enthusiasm. Even the bright colours of her clothes couldn't disguise how miserable she was.

Flora said hello, but Sylvie moved straight into position. 'Right,' she said, in a low voice so that Tilda wouldn't overhear, 'we got here on Tuesday at 6.40 p.m. We rang the bell and Tilda let us in. The others hadn't arrived.'

'We came and stood here,' Flora said, taking over the story. She moved to the refectory table. They now stood between the cabinet and Tilda's desk. The entrance was beyond the cabinet. Flora tried to remember every second of that evening: what she'd said, what she'd done, what she'd seen. 'It was getting dark outside; the market was packed up. You said something to Tilda about a sleepover in the shop.'

Sylvie nodded. 'That's right. Then Benedict came in.'

'But we didn't know he was Benedict.'

'Not until Tilda made a big fuss of him.'

'Well, he is her nephew.'

Sylvie looked at the door. Flora followed her gaze. They both remembered Benedict sweeping open the door, beaming at Tilda, announcing himself to the shop and everything in it. Even them, until he realised they weren't customers.

What had he done next?

Taken off his scarf. Hugged Tilda. Accepted the offer of tea. Had he gone near the cabinet before Piotr, Minnie and Andrew arrived?

'You know, I really don't think he did,' Flora said.

'No, me neither.'

It was deeply frustrating. They had had the suspect right under their noses, but hadn't seen him do anything remotely suspicious.

'Aunt Tilda!'

Flora and Sylvie exchanged looks. Benedict's shout had come from the back of the shop.

'He's here,' Sylvie hissed.

They heard him bustle closer.

'I've got another brochure for Spain. The climate is so much more forgiving. Oh.' He stopped when he saw the twins. He gave a tight shake of his head. 'Tilda tells me you mean well, but this shop isn't a playground. I'm not sure you should be here. Unless you want to buy something?' he added hopefully.

'They're not doing any harm, dear,' Tilda said. She patted Benedict's arm. 'And the shop is so quiet.' She picked up a leaflet from the desk. Flora saw photos of white houses with terracotta roofs on the front.

Benedict turned his back on them very deliberately and leaned over the leaflet. 'That one looks lovely,' he said. 'If I wasn't going to be so busy here, I'd join you.'

'Are you going on holiday?' Flora asked, stepping closer.

'Something like that,' Tilda replied. 'Benedict here is going to run the shop for me, so I can rest.'

'You're giving him the shop?' Sylvie exclaimed.

Tilda opened the leaflet and stared at the pictures of sandy beaches and sapphire-blue seas. 'It was always going to be his, once I retire. It is a family business, after all. It was my dad's before me, and his dad's before that. This is just handing it over a little earlier than planned, that's all.'

'When?' Flora asked.

Benedict stepped between Flora and Tilda with another leaflet. He gave it to his aunt. 'No time like the present,' he said breezily. 'It's been a difficult time for Aunt Tilda.'

'The present?' Sylvie said. 'You mean, like, right now?'

'The next few days, yes,' Benedict said. 'What do you think of Tuscany, Aunt Tilda?'

'I expect it's very nice at this time of year, thank you, dear.'

Flora raised her eyebrow. Benedict was moving fast. He was practically shoving Tilda out of the door!

But how would they prove it?

She was about to speak when she heard a trilling sound come from Benedict's pocket. His mobile. He answered it smoothly: 'Benedict Meeke speaking.' Then he listened, making agreeing murmurs and mutters.

He hung up and gave Tilda a broad smile. 'It's been a wonderful afternoon getting to know the ins and outs of the shop, but I'm afraid I must leave.'

Tilda nodded. 'Of course, dear, it's getting late. We can sort out the details tomorrow.'

Benedict dropped a kiss on his aunt's cheek and picked up his jacket and scarf from a nearby chair. He nodded curtly at the twins, then he was gone with a tinkling of the bell.

Flora looked at Sylvie and tried her very best to send her thoughts into her twin's brain. Luckily, they didn't have to rely on paranormal activity, as it seemed Sylvie was thinking the exact same thing. 'We have to go too, Tilda,' she said. 'We'll probably see you again tomorrow. Bye!'

Sylvie grabbed Flora's wrist and together they raced out of the shop.

Just in time to see Benedict disappear around the corner, heading towards the end of Marsh Road, where the gallery and grill restaurant stood.

Sylvie picked up the pace, with Flora close behind.

They were gaining on him now. But he didn't look back. He was intent on his destination.

Theatre Square.

A bench.

With a woman sitting on it.

Her little dog barked. She stood, opened her arms. Benedict stepped into her embrace. They kissed.

'Yuck,' Flora said.

'Wow,' Sylvie said.

Chapter Eighteen

Piotr and Minnie watched from behind a tree as Benedict and Miranda walked away, arms linked together.

'Wow,' Piotr said, 'this changes everything.'

'Yes –' Minnie leaned against the bark '– a suspect with a motive but no opportunity working with a suspect with opportunity but no motive suddenly looks, well, very guilty.'

'Exactly.'

'Hey, there are the twins. Flora! Sylvie!' Minnie glanced to check Benedict and Miranda were far enough away before waving to catch the girls' attention.

Flora and Sylvie ran over. 'Did you see? Benedict and Miranda were snogging!' Sylvie said.

'We saw.'

'Should we follow them?'

Piotr looked up at the darkening sky. Rain clouds were

scudding in and night was on its way. 'I think we wait until morning. Then go, all together, to Miranda's house. She might be more willing to talk. After all, it's Benedict who wants Tilda's shop.'

Flora pulled the edges of her coat tighter. 'Will Andrew come? He's been worried about his mum.'

'He wants to lift the curse,' Piotr said. 'He'll come.'

'Tomorrow, then,' Minnie said. 'We can crack this case wide open.'

Andrew heard moth-wing taps on the front door. Mum was in her room, not asleep, but resting. He opened the front door. Piotr stood there, his eyes flashing with excitement. His hair was damp from rain.

'Did I disturb your mum?' Piotr asked, glancing over Andrew's shoulder.

'No. She's OK.'

'Good. You'll never guess which Honourable Lady and junk-shop-owner-to-be are dating!'

'No!' Andrew felt his heart flutter. Was it true? Miranda and Benedict were an item? 'They set the curse together?'

Piotr wiped his forehead with the back of his sleeve. 'It looks to me like there's not so much a curse,' he said, 'as

124

two people conspiring to steal an antiques business off a poor old lady.'

The paint around the door frame flaked against his fingertips. What did that mean for Mum? If there wasn't really a curse? Why had she got so ill all of a sudden? If there was no curse, then whatever had happened to Mum was more serious than he'd thought. His grip tightened. Was she ever going to get better?

'Are you all right?' Piotr asked.

'Yes, fine. I've got to go.'

'But, wait. In the morning, do you want to come to Miranda's?'

'Sure. Yes.'

Andrew raised his hand in a swift goodbye, then closed the door.

Rain hammered against the windowpanes all night. Andrew hardly slept. He wondered whether Mum was able to rest at all. He must have dropped off at some point, because when he opened his eyes, he found he'd wrapped himself in his duvet like he was the filling of a Cornish pasty. He struggled free and got up. Yesterday's clothes were on the floor. He swapped pyjamas for black jeans and a check shirt.

There was no sound from Mum's room, so he peeked inside. She was curled up, hugging the pillow, fast asleep.

He didn't want to wake her, so he just closed the door and went to make breakfast for himself. He spooned cereal into his mouth and wondered what Piotr's plan was. If he proved there was no curse, and Benedict and Miranda were behind Tilda's vision and the broken goblets, then where did that leave Mum?

He rinsed the bowl.

There was a tap at the door. Piotr.

'Wait there,' he told him. 'I need to leave a note for Mum.'

In the kitchen he scrawled a message and stuck it to the fridge. 'Have been kidnapped by aliens, send Luke Skywalker (not really, am out with Piotr). Love you, A'. That should make her laugh.

Then, he headed out.

'Nice accessories,' Piotr said as they climbed down the stairwell.

Andrew looked down to where Piotr was pointing. His jeans. He still had a couple of sparkly hair clips secured against his pocket. 'Thanks,' he said. 'You can borrow them whenever you want.'

'We're meeting the others on Miranda's street.'

They walked together along Marsh Road, through Theatre Square and along the tree-lined streets that marked the start of the posh part of town to Old Wynd House. A few windows in houses nearby glowed, lit by lamps. The morning was dark and dingy. Rainwater still glistened in murky puddles. The scene reminded Andrew of an old film he'd seen with Oliver and Fagin in it.

The girls were already there, bundled in thick coats and scarves.

Piotr said hello, then he stomped up to the door and thwacked the knocker hard.

He waited.

There was no flurry of barks. No sound of any kind. He knocked again. Nothing.

'Our suspect is missing,' Piotr said finally.

'Just out,' Flora said.

'We can wait,' Minnie said.

Andrew eyed the sky. The rain clouds looked like tarpaulin flapping in a strong breeze. He would wait, as long as it didn't start to rain.

Piotr found a tin can and they kept warm by playing a game of kickabout. The road had hardly any traffic, so they were able to race around shooting at constantly moving goals. No one kept score. No one kept an eye out for Miranda, either, after a while. By the time they stopped the game, the clouds had passed and the sky overhead was a sparkling blue. The sun had moved a long way across the morning sky when Flora picked up the very battered tin can and said, 'She's home!'

A black taxicab pulled into the mews and sat with its motor running. Then the door opened and Miranda stepped out. Bruiser was tucked under her arm. She waved goodbye to the driver and then stepped towards her house. She paused when she saw the gang.

'Oh,' she said. 'Tilda's helpers. And friends.'

'Hello,' Andrew said brightly. 'We were hoping you might have time to talk to us.'

'Certainly. Any friend of Tilda's is a friend of mine. Come on in.'

Miranda held the door open as they trooped inside. Bruiser gave Andrew a yelp and lick as he passed. Andrew hoped that if Benedict was guilty, and if Miranda was his accomplice, then Bruiser was completely innocent.

In the kitchen, Miranda put the dog down and it clattered around welcoming them all.

'We've been helping Tilda with a problem she's been having, and we wondered if you might be able to help too,' Flora said.

Miranda sat on one of the high stools near a black marble counter. 'If I can, I will.'

'Tilda has had some very strange experiences recently. Someone has been trying to frighten her.'

Andrew was very interested to see that Miranda blushed slightly at Flora's words.

'Really?' she said.

'Yes. She thought she saw something appear in front of her.'

Miranda's face turned a deeper shade of red. Everyone had noticed. Miranda's hands flew to cover her cheeks, but already it was too late. She couldn't look more guilty if she tried.

'And what,' Andrew boomed, 'do you know about that?'

'Me?' Miranda squeaked. Then she shook her head. 'Oh, it's no use. I'm terrible at spying and sneaking around. I didn't mean to hurt her, I swear.'

'So,' Andrew said, 'you admit it! You set the curse!'

Miranda looked confused. 'Of course not. I had nothing to do with anything. But I wasn't honest with Tilda. You see, I've been dating her nephew. She's his closest relative, but he's never introduced us. I was curious, so I went to look. I didn't really want to buy a sofa. I just wanted to see what she was like. I'm sorry, I should have been honest. And now Benny is so worried about his aunt, and I feel terrible for snooping. Do you think I should tell them?'

Andrew gazed at Miranda.

Would someone who was embarrassed about snooping really set a curse on an old woman and her shop?

Just then, the doorbell rang.

'Oh!' Miranda said brightly. 'That will be Benny. He was getting lunch.'

She disappeared into the hallway.

'She doesn't seem like much of an accomplice!' Andrew hissed.

Flora and Piotr shook their heads.

'She's going to be so upset when she finds out her boyfriend is trying to swindle an old lady out of her business!' Sylvie said.

In moments, Miranda was back, this time with Benedict on her arm. 'We've got visitors, Benny,' she said brightly.

He took one look at the gang and his face darkened. 'No,' he said. 'No, no, no. These children get everywhere. I can't turn around in this town without finding one of them nosing around.'

Andrew glared at Benedict. He was the one who had set up the curse. And after that, Mum had got ill again. This was all his fault. 'You have to stop what you're doing, right now!' Andrew said.

'I'm cooking eggs!' Benedict said, holding up a carrier bag.

'Not that. The curse. We know that you were the one who sent Tilda the mummy. And I'm not leaving here until I have an anti-curse serum, or whatever it is I need to make Mum well again.'

Andrew felt Piotr lay a warning hand on his arm.

Was he going too far? He often only knew he'd gone too far because someone told him afterwards.

'My aunt,' Benedict said slowly, 'is under a lot of stress at the moment. She has always had a fanciful imagination and I really don't appreciate you fuelling it.'

'We don't all believe in the curse,' Flora said quickly.

Judas!

Andrew clutched his chest as though she had stabbed him in the heart. Flora rolled her eyes in his general direction.

'Well, we don't,' Flora said simply. 'But we do believe that someone wants Tilda to believe in the curse. That someone is trying to make it look as though the mummy brought bad luck with it. Someone made Tilda think she was seeing visions. They made the crystal goblets shatter. Someone with access to Egyptian artefacts and someone with a motive to get Tilda to leave her shop.'

Andrew eyed Benedict meaningfully.

'Me?' His index finger jabbed at himself in alarm. 'You can't mean me? I would never do anything to hurt my aunt. She's been like a mother to me. As soon as I heard she was in trouble I went rushing over there. But until she called I had no idea there was anything wrong. Did I, snookums?' He looked over at Miranda.

'It's true,' she said. 'Tilda called completely out of the blue. We had no idea about the so-called curse.'

'You said your grandfather's Egyptian relics were stored upstairs?' Piotr asked.

'That's right. In the loft.'

'Well, would you mind if we take a look?'

'We've got nothing to hide,' Miranda said sharply.

'Then you have no reason to not show us,' Flora replied firmly.

Chapter Nineteen

Miranda led them from the kitchen, up a wide staircase, then up a slightly smaller staircase, to the third floor of the house.

At the top of the stairs was a brown door, bolted shut. Miranda pulled back the bolt and fumbled for a light switch.

They all followed her inside.

It was an attic space, like something from a children's story. Dark shadows hid ancient toys – a tricycle, a rocking horse. Suitcases and trunks were piled high, stickered with scenes of Cairo and Singapore and Rio de Janeiro. The air tingled with dust. There was barely enough room for all of them to stand, despite the fact that the attic stretched the whole length of the house.

'I've been thinking about turning this into a fifth bedroom, with an en suite, in case we need the space one day.' There was a slight rosing of Miranda's cheeks as she said this; her eyes darted away from Benedict. 'But I haven't done much about it. So, the mess up here is pretty much how my family left it. I think Grandpa Douglas's stuff is over here.'

She walked to a far corner of the space, careful to keep her cream cashmere clothes away from the smears of cobwebs or grime. She pulled her cardigan closer to her body. Andrew followed, not at all bothered by the dirt and dust. Every good detective had to be willing to get dirty sometimes. He could hear the others following behind, the floor creaking under the weight of their steps.

'Here,' Miranda said.

Grandpa Douglas's stuff was arranged on some rickety grey shelving. It reminded Andrew of an exhibition he'd seen at a war museum. Old box cameras, white hats with burgundy bands, a briefcase and gilt-edged cigar trays. One or two much older objects: a marble statue only twenty centimetres high showing a dancing woman; a clay jar fired with a dark crumbly coating that looked old enough to be at Stonehenge.

'What's that?' Flora pointed to an empty space on the shelf.

'Nothing,' Miranda said.

'The dust, there's a gap in the dust.'

Andrew could see what she meant. There was a darker rectangle clearly visible on the shelf where something had been disturbed. About the size of a violin case.

'Oh,' Miranda said. Her hand covered her mouth.

'What used to be there?' Piotr asked, more insistently.

'Oh dear,' Miranda said.

'What was it?' Minnie demanded.

'A mummified cat,' Miranda whispered.

'Miranda?' It was Benedict who whispered her name. That one word was filled with fear and hurt and confusion.

'Benedict, I wouldn't ... I didn't ... you can't think ...'

Andrew looked from one to the other. Miranda confused and hurt. Benedict confused and angry.

Which one of them was guilty?

Which one of them had moved the mummy?

'I think we should go back downstairs and talk about this,' Flora said.

Then, in the seeping shadows, Benedict's phone rang. He pulled it from his pocket and answered gruffly. 'Yes ... slow down ... I can't hear you ... wait, I'm coming. I'm on my way.' He hung up and raked his fingers through his hair. When he dropped his hands, his face looked tired and worn. 'A fire,' he said. 'There's been a fire at Aunt Tilda's.'

Chapter Twenty

'Is Tilda all right? Is she hurt?' Miranda was the first person to ask, but the others clamoured with questions too.

Benedict held up his hands, his phone still cradled in his palm. 'That was Tilda. She's OK, but there's been some damage to the shop. I have to go.'

There was no time to think. Everyone piled out of the attic, down the stairs and out of the front door. The rain had returned, streaking down in grey ribbons. Miranda stopped for long enough to swipe a set of keys from a bowl on the hall table.

'My car!' she said.

There was a nippy little sports car parked under a shelter. She pressed her key fob and the car chirruped. It was a tight squeeze in the back seat, but they all managed to get in. Miranda got behind the wheel, with Benedict sitting anxiously in the passenger seat. Andrew could see his knuckles were white where he gripped the edge of his seat.

'Hold on,' Miranda said, easing the car into gear and flipping on the wipers.

'We can do better than that,' Flora said from Piotr's knee, clicking the seat belt into place over them both.

The car engine revved like a thoroughbred in a stall then glided out, crunching over loose stones and gravel. Nestled in the curve of the seat, Andrew smelled leather and a hint of Miranda's perfume.

The car glided through the streets as though it were a ghost. Almost soundless, inside and out.

They were too worried by what they might find at the shop to speak.

The car couldn't go all the way down Marsh Road, so Miranda pulled up at the bollards which stopped the traffic. 'You go. I'll park the car and find you in a minute. Go and see that your aunt is all right.'

Benedict stretched his long legs out of the car and pulled his seat forward so that the gang could clamber out after him.

Some confused street lamps had flickered on and the few stall holders who had set up that morning were hastily packing their wares away. The road looked sleek and wet under the oily glow. There weren't many people about. No fire engines. No blaze illuminating frightened faces. They walked closer.

The junk shop was shut up in darkness.

The glass in the front door was shattered. Sharp teeth were left, jagged in the frame. Beyond that, black.

But there was a light on in the salon next door.

Andrew could see Minnie's mum, and Tilda sitting in the window seat, looking small and shaken.

Benedict led the way, his long legs outstripping even Minnie. He rushed into the salon, and was holding his aunt in a hug in seconds. 'Are you all right?' he asked frantically. 'Do you need to see a doctor?'

'She's not hurt,' Mrs Adesina said. 'Just shaken.'

Minnie's dad came from the back of the salon, carrying a steaming mug. 'Tea,' he said firmly, 'with lots of sugar.'

Benedict let Tilda go, so that she could take the tea. But, Andrew noticed, he left his hand on his aunt's arm, in just the same way that Andrew had touched his mum while she was in hospital. Just a tiny touch, to remind the other person that you were there for them.

Benedict wasn't acting like a person who had laid a curse to steal a shop.

'Could you tell us what happened?' Piotr asked Mrs Adesina.

'Please?' Benedict added.

Flora tugged off her trusty backpack and pulled out her notebook and pencil, ready to record everything they were told. Minnie dropped into a seat at the nail bar. Sylvie stood behind her. Andrew and Piotr joined Tilda and Benedict in the window seat.

Mrs Adesina looked from Minnie to Flora to Tilda and back. 'Are you children getting involved with something again?'

Minnie gave a small shrug.

'I don't like it,' Mrs Adesina said. 'It is dangerous. Look at what happened today.'

Benedict leaned forward. 'Please, can you tell me what happened? I need to know.' His voice shook.

Mrs Adesina sighed. 'All right. But I don't want any of you children getting into trouble. Is that clear?'

Andrew wondered exactly how they could not get into trouble when they were actually cursed. After all, it wasn't as though they could just decide not to be, was it? It was more like being ill. He didn't bother to reply to Mrs Adesina, and she seemed to take their silence as agreement.

'Well, it was just me here. The whole road has been very quiet today because of the weather,' Mrs Adesina said. 'I was sweeping; the music was on low. And that's when I heard it. A smash, then a rustling, crackling noise. I looked outside and smelled the smoke. I knew there was a fire. There's an extinguisher right next to our front door, so I dropped the broom and grabbed it. I could see the fire then, just inside the door to Tilda's shop. It was still small, but fierce. I pulled out the pin on the extinguisher and sprayed water right at it.'

'Mum!' Minnie said in awe. 'You're a hero!'

'She is,' Tilda whispered. 'She saved the shop and she saved me. I was out the back. I had no idea the fire was there until I heard Mrs Adesina shouting my name.'

Andrew wiped his palms against the front of his jeans. Tilda had been inside the building when the fire started? He swallowed. His throat felt so dry it was as if he had inhaled smoke.

'How did it start? Do you know?' Flora asked.

Tilda raised her head to look at Mrs Adesina. 'I don't know,' she said, so softly they could barely hear her.

'The moment the flames were out, I got Tilda through the front door; we locked it and came straight here. She called Benedict and that's been that. We were too busy getting clear of the danger to worry about what caused it.'

'Very sensible too,' Benedict said. 'I can't thank you enough for what you've done for my aunt.'

The door to the salon opened and Miranda walked in. She took a look at Tilda, then seemed to relax in relief. The tightness around her mouth softened.

Was she relieved because she had nothing to do with the fire and Tilda was safe?

Or was she relieved because she had set the fire and hadn't known Tilda was still inside?

But that didn't make sense. They had been with Benedict and Miranda when the fire started. There was no way they could have slipped away from the attic, started the fire and then come back again without the gang noticing. It was just impossible.

Yet another impossible thing.

Andrew felt his skin shiver. The curse was still going strong. And this time, Tilda had come way too close to getting hurt.

'Can we see the shop?' Flora asked.

'We should call the police,' Benedict said. 'This has gone too far now. We need to find out what's been going on.'

'The police?' Minnie said; the disappointment was clear in her voice.

'Yes,' her mum snapped. 'That is absolutely the best idea. We should have done it as soon as we put out the fire. It's time to call the police. And it's time that you all stopped investigating, if that's what you've been doing. People who set fires don't care who they hurt.'

'But, Mum!' Minnie began.

'"But Mum" nothing,' Mrs Adesina said. 'It's time for you children to go on home and leave this to the professionals. Come on, you've been out all day. Your parents will be worried. This stops now and you leave it to the police. Understand?'

Minnie sighed. Even Flora looked cross as she closed her notebook.

But a direct order from Mrs Adesina was very difficult to ignore.

Difficult, but not impossible, Andrew thought.

Chapter Twenty-One

Outside the salon, the twins looked as miserable as the weather. Flora sidled up to the door of the junk shop and peered in through the shattered glass.

'The carpet's all scorched and damp,' she said. 'And it smells like ash and burnt paper.'

'Home!' Mrs Adesina yelled from the salon doorway.

Piotr smiled and waved. 'We're on our way!' he said.

They crossed the road. A misty rain wetted their eyelashes and made the street look like a filtered photograph.

'We'd better go,' Flora said. 'I hope it's Jimmy who comes to investigate.'

'I'm sure it will be,' Piotr said. 'It's on his beat. And we can tell him everything we know about the case.'

Sylvie shook her head. 'We don't know anything. Think about it. If the fire was set deliberately – and we don't know it was yet – then it can't have been Miranda or Benedict, because we were with them the whole time.'

The cat.

It had to be.

This was proof. If the humans hadn't done it, then it must have been the evil, sinister powers of the Egyptian mummy. 'The curse,' Andrew said gravely.

'Oh, don't start that again,' Sylvie snapped.

Andrew turned to Flora.

'Sorry, but I agree with Sylvie,' Flora whispered.

Andrew looked to Piotr. Surely he was ready to listen now?

Piotr shrugged.

Oh.

Andrew pushed his hands deep into his pockets. None of the others were on his side.

And it was a question of sides.

He could do something about a curse. He could burn the mummy, or hide it, or give it away, or communicate with it. He could fix whatever it was the cat was after and, by doing that, fix Mum.

If there was no curse to lift, then Mum had got worse for no reason. She needed him again, in the way she had right after her accident, and there was no explanation for it.

Andrew would never, ever, ever say so out loud, but the idea of having to look after Mum forever felt so hard.

He forced himself to smile. 'Well,' he said, as lightly as he could manage, 'Sylvie's phone thought there was a ghost. And I trust her phone – it's an iPhantom.'

Piotr smiled and clapped his hand on Andrew's shoulder. 'Shall we get on back?'

Andrew smiled again, glad that the spitting rain gave him an excuse to wipe his eyes. 'No, you go. I've got to pick up a few things for tea.'

'I can wait?'

'No, really. We can decide what we want to do tomorrow. Perhaps talk to Jimmy.'

Andrew kept his smile plastered in place until the twins and Piotr had disappeared from view. Then he clamped his lips together tightly. He was not going to cry. He waited until the wave of misery passed.

He wandered through the skeleton frames of the empty stalls. Almost everyone was gone.

But there was one stall which was still open. A light shone from Elspeth's fortune-telling tent.

Andrew paused. He fingered Mum's hair clip in his pocket.

Elspeth had seen his mother in her tarot cards.

He found himself moving towards the canvas door. This time the tent was lit with little battery-powered lanterns. It made the inside feel warm and welcoming, as though it was something from *The Arabian Nights*.

'Hello!' Elspeth said from her pile of cushions. Her cat was curled up next to her. 'It's you! I've been decorating; what do you think? I got a great deal on the lanterns.'

'It's very nice.'

'Oh, you do sound down in the dumps. Come in, come in. Sit.'

Andrew dropped on to the cushions wearily. He wished he could just curl up and go to sleep like the cat.

Elspeth pulled her stack of cloth-swaddled cards from under the low table. 'Is it another reading you want?'

Andrew shook his head. 'I don't think so.'

'Well, I haven't got a crystal ball. So, if it's the future you're after, it will have to be the cards. Unless it's about that curse you were worried about. Did you get to the bottom of that?'

Andrew picked at the fringing of one of the cushions. 'No. But I wondered if you might be able to. You could tell me if the cat's spirit is haunting Tilda and Mum, couldn't you? Please?'

Elspeth looked suddenly serious. 'Did you talk to it?'

'Yes, it smashed the junk shop up. And now it's trying to burn the place down. And no one will listen to me.'

Elspeth shoved her cards away and yanked herself upright. 'The junk shop? I love that place. Come on, let's see what we can find.'

She swept out over the cushions like a rugby player charging for a tackle – head down, shoulders set, her skirts swishing behind her. She pulled a shawl over her head against the rain and stepped outside. Andrew scrambled to keep up. She tied the canvas closed and stomped over to Meeke's.

The shop was in darkness. There was no sign of anyone in the salon either. Perhaps Benedict had taken Tilda home.

But the door to Meeke's opened as Elspeth pushed the handle.

Was there someone in the shop? Or had the cat left the door open? Were they being lured into a trap? It reeked of smoke. Cold embers crunched under his feet.

'Hello?' a frightened voice wavered. He heard footsteps.

A shape coming closer. Stepping into the space between shadows.

It was Miranda.

'Hello,' she said to Elspeth, 'we're closed, I'm afraid. Tilda isn't here. I'm just waiting for the police.'

'I'm Elspeth,' Elspeth said, as though Miranda hadn't spoken.

'She's basically Ghostbusters,' Andrew added.

'Miranda.'

'I'm here about this cat. The one Andrew suspects is causing the destruction.'

Miranda looked around the space, as if searching for a satisfactory reply. 'I don't know if it's a good –'

'It's just over here,' Andrew said, before Miranda could ask them to leave. He stepped over to the shelves and lifted down the black case.

'Oh!' Miranda said. 'That looks an awful lot like Grandpa Douglas's case. How on earth did it end up here?' She switched on a desk lamp, which cast a warm glow over the case.

Andrew undid the clasps and lifted the lid. 'You can take it back, if you like.'

'Not if it's cursed,' Miranda said.

'You think it is?' Andrew asked hopefully.

'There are lots of strange things in the world which we can't explain,' she said.

'Was your grandad cursed?' Andrew asked suddenly. If he'd found it and brought it from Egypt, it stood to reason he'd be cursed. 'Did he die in a freak accident involving roller skates and a tiger?' he asked Miranda.

'No. He died in bed aged eighty-seven.'

Oh.

'Maybe he was miserable and lonely and wandered the world alone and misunderstood?'

Miranda shook her head. 'He was married three times. His third wife was a jazz singer. He died holding her hand.'

Andrew had to admit, Douglas didn't sound cursed.

They looked inside the case.

Andrew lifted the letter, which lay on top of the tissue paper. It looked more yellow than it had done. Smoke damage? He unfolded it. He caught a faint whiff of burning. Definitely smoke damage. The V-S-Y watermark stood out much more boldly. He put it aside and lifted the tissue paper.

'Oh, it's uglier than I remember,' Miranda said.

'Stand aside,' Elspeth said.

Andrew moved, to give her room. She held out her

hands above the shrivelled, bandaged form and stretched her fingers. Her breathing slowed. The seconds passed. She stood, perfectly still, like a statue of a saint.

Finally, she dropped her hands.

'Sorry, kid, I've got nothing. That cat is dead as roadkill. Whatever it is bothering Tilda, it isn't that feline.'

Chapter Twenty-Two

Mum looked pale. Her bedside light cast deep shadows across her cheeks. Andrew put a glass of water down for her.

'Thanks, sweetheart. Listen. Three across, six letters, a faint whisper, starts with "M-something-R"?' She held her pen above her bumper book of crosswords hopefully.

'I have no idea. We should make an appointment at the doctor,' Andrew said.

'Why? Are you poorly?'

'No. But you are.'

'Just tired. Nothing a good night's sleep won't fix.'

Andrew made a noise that was disagreeing without arguing.

She smiled at him. Then gasped.

'Are you OK?'

'Murmur! Three across is murmur!'

He left her to it and went to get ready for bed.

Pyjamas, toothbrush, toothpaste, a tiny bit of singing into the toothbrush to classic pop tunes. Then actually cleaning his teeth. His brush slowed as he stared at himself in the mirror. He'd taken off his glasses and the reflected image was blurry. Something was bothering him.

Something to do with three across.

What was it?

Not the clue. Or the answer. Mum probably had that right. But something about it was making his brain feel a little itchy. As though he had left the house but forgotten to lock the front door.

M-something-R?

Then it hit him.

The letter he'd lifted from the mummy's case that evening – the watermark had been damaged by the smoke. It said V-something-S-something-Y! Tilda had thought it said Valley, because of Valley of the Kings. But it couldn't. It didn't fit. The smoke had scorched the S and made it visible.

He spat in the sink and dropped his toothbrush into the cup.

V-something-S-something-Y.

What could that be? Was it a clue?

Vosey? Vesay? Visey? They didn't mean anything to him. They weren't even real words.

Vusay? Vasey?

He paused.

Vasey.

That was ringing the tiniest bell imaginable. He'd seen that somewhere.

Andrew splashed water on his face, rinsing away stray blobs of toothpaste. He dried his hands, patted his cheeks.

Vasey.

On Marsh Road.

The construction firm who were redeveloping the building opposite Meeke's were called Vasey. He'd tried to make an anagram from their name a few days ago, and failed.

But he was sure he hadn't failed this time.

The letter was a fake.

Someone had used Vasey Construction's business paper to write the note inside the mummy's case. They hadn't noticed the watermark.

But who?

And why?

Was he right?

Andrew left the bathroom and headed to his bedroom. He paused by the phone in the hallway. He had the tingling feeling he got when a case was getting hotter. But maybe he was just catching a cold from being out in the rain.

He needed a second opinion.

It was just about not too late to call Piotr.

Before he could talk himself out of it, he picked up the phone and dialled. Piotr's mum answered, and, though she didn't sound very pleased about it, she took the phone through to Piotr, who was reading in bed.

'Hi,' Andrew said. 'You busy?'

'I've got the latest edition of *Batman*. But no, not really. What's up?'

'I think I've got something.' He explained quickly about V-something-S-something-Y.

Piotr made some doubtful noises. 'Maybe it's just a coincidence? I mean, the letter looked really old. What makes you think that it has anything to do with a construction company?'

'There are builders right there! On Marsh Road.' Another flash went off in his mind. 'And Miranda's kitchen is lovely!'

Piotr laughed. 'What's that got to do with anything?'

'Builders! I bet a million dollars that if we asked Miranda which builders made her extension, she'd say Vasey. And I bet that they went up to the loft poking around her grandad's stuff. If Benedict and Miranda didn't touch the mummy, then someone must have. We should ask Miranda!'

Piotr sighed. 'And we will. But in the morning.'

'I could try and call her now?'

'It's late. It can wait until morning. And so can you.'

'I don't know if I can.'

'Well, try. Goodnight.' And with that, Piotr hung up.

Chapter Twenty-Three

Andrew put the receiver back in its cradle and walked slowly to his bedroom. The second opinion hadn't gone so well. Piotr wasn't convinced. But Andrew was sure his hunch was right. Builders had been in Miranda's house – they had opportunity to steal the mummy. They had access to the watermarked notepaper to fake the note about the curse.

He didn't know – yet – how they had made the vision appear in front of Tilda, or the crystal goblets smash, but he bet they had done it.

He sat down heavily on his bed, feeling the springs bounce beneath him.

If Vasey Construction had done it, then there was no curse. Flora was right. Which meant that whatever was wrong with Mum had nothing to do with Meeke's.

He swung his legs up and lay on top of the duvet. The pillow felt flat and uncomfortable beneath his head.

Mum was sick again.

That's what his hunch meant.

Worry about Mum was like a spiky creature living inside him. Sometimes it was dormant, hibernating, and he could forget about it for a while. Other times it was awake, active, scratching at his insides and making him feel ill with it all. He screwed up his eyes tight and curled on his side.

Mum was sick.

Eventually, he fell asleep.

He woke suddenly. His eyes shot open, his heart pounding. The fug of dreams still clouded his mind, but he knew that something had woken him. What? He sat up. The room was cold now, and without his duvet he shivered. What had disturbed him? Was it just the cold?

Then, he heard something.

Mum, crying out. Not his name, not even a word – it was a cry of fear.

He stood and rushed to her room.

The grey shapes of night-time made Mum's room look like a cave, dark and chilly. Mum was still asleep, but he could make out the lines on her face, her forehead creased and her eyes screwed shut against whatever was haunting her. She whispered something, then whimpered.

He paced to her side. 'Mum, it's all right, it's all right.' He tried to sound soothing, but he could hear the worry in his own voice. More firm, he decided, more confident. 'It's all right,' he tried again.

Mum stirred. Her eyelids flittered open. 'Oh.' The sound was anguished. 'Oh, Andrew.'

He reached out and stroked her face. 'Another bad dream?'

She nodded.

'What was it? Can you remember?'

She pressed her eyes closed. She didn't answer.

Fire. He knew it would be the fire. He took her hand and squeezed it. He could feel the bones in her palms through her paper-thin skin.

'We should see the doctor,' he said, 'they might be able to help you sleep better.'

Mum shook her head. 'There's no medicine for bad dreams,' she said. 'There's no medicine for bad luck. What happened happened. Only time will make it better.'

But how much time if a year wasn't enough? And how long would she stay cooped up in the flat?

'Do you want to try Meeke's again?' Andrew asked. 'Maybe some fresh air would help? We could go tomorrow.'

'No!' Mum snatched her hand away. 'Sorry, but no. I need more time.'

'OK. Do you need anything now? A drink?'

'No, I'm tired. I'm sorry I woke you.'

'Well, don't let the bed bugs bite,' he said, standing up.

'Don't. I'll dream about monster insects too.' He was glad she was able to smile.

As he turned to leave, he caught sight of her crossword book on the bedside table.

All over again, he remembered Vasey.

He went to his own room and got under the duvet. He lay in the dark, staring up at the ceiling. It was much harder to fall asleep this time. He checked the clock beside his bed. Nearly midnight. Vasey Construction. They had opportunity. There was physical evidence linking them to the scene of the crime. He wondered, for a second, whether faking a curse was a crime. Even if it wasn't, breaking goblets was.

He should just leave it to the police. Tilda had called them now.

It had nothing to do with him and Mum any more. She wasn't cursed, she was ill.

He should leave it be.

He turned on his side to get more comfortable. The bed felt like bricks underneath him. He tried the other way. Rocks. He lay on his back. He wasn't going to get back to sleep.

Vasey Construction wanted to scare Tilda. Why? Did they have a motive?

He tapped out a rhythm on his duvet with his finger-tips. Why would they want to make people believe the shop was cursed?

It didn't make any sense. It was like a crossword with clues missing.

He got up and pulled on his clothes.

He would just nip out for five minutes, just for a bit of fresh air. It would help him sleep. He'd go down to the play park, just for a second. In the hallway he got his coat and keys. He thought about checking on Mum. But he didn't want to wake her. And anyway, she'd just ask him why he was dressed and he knew there was no way she'd let him out at this time of night.

As he passed the phone, he stopped. His eyes landed on the phone directory. It wouldn't hurt to know where Vasey Construction was. He wouldn't go there. Not alone. Not at night. But it wouldn't hurt to know the address. He flicked the pages quickly, looking for the letter 'V'.

Vasey Construction was on the road that led out towards the hospital.

Maybe a ten- or fifteen-minute walk.

But he wouldn't go there. What would be the point? No one would even be there at midnight.

It was a stupid idea.

Andrew let himself out of the flat.

Chapter Twenty-Four

Outside seemed to have forgotten that it was nearly spring. The air was sharp with cold. The tree branches clattered together in the breeze. He could hear a car alarm sounding off in the distance. There was no one around. A sudden movement made him gasp, before the slinking figure of a fox scurried towards the bins.

He walked towards the play park, his shoulders hunched against the chill. But, at the gate, he found his feet continued walking. Out on to the pavement, to Marsh Road, before turning right. It was better to keep moving, he thought, than to swing back and forth. His hands plunged into his pockets. A few cars whizzed by, taxis mostly. A late-night bus rumbled to a stop and a handful of people got off, joking and laughing with each other. He kept his head down and slipped past unnoticed.

At the main road, he turned left.

He was halfway to the hospital, he realised with a blink of surprise. He hadn't meant to come this way at all.

But seeing as he was here.

What harm could it do to stand outside an empty office, looking at the name plate? No harm at all, he decided. And as soon as he'd seen it, he'd turn right back around and go to bed and Mum would never even know he'd left the flat.

He picked up the pace, walking quickly, keeping an eye on the building numbers as he passed. Vasey Construction was at 230. He was in the low 100s. The shutters were down on newsagents and sandwich shops and cafes. Low-rise blocks of flats were mostly in darkness. Even the road seemed quiet. He reached the 200s. His pace slowed. He was checking the name plates now.

He reached 230. A single-storey white building was set back from the road by a small car park. A neat sign advertised 'Vasey Construction, Head Office' behind a low wall. There was a car in the car park. Behind the low building there were rusty yellow construction trucks.

And, in the building itself, a light on in the office.

Chapter Twenty-Five

Andrew held his breath, stuck to the spot.

He hadn't expected anyone to be in Vasey Construction. He hadn't planned on investigating without the others. Or even on leaving the flat. He hadn't planned any of it, and yet, here he was.

As he walked across the car park, his trainer caught a stone and sent it chittering into the darkness. It sounded loud. He glanced about. He could see no one.

At the bottom of a short flight of steps, he paused. Was this a good idea? Before he had time to think he was at the top of the steps, ringing the buzzer.

For a moment, there was no sound, besides an ambulance siren at the far end of the road. Then, behind the door, he heard someone rattling the lock. The door opened.

'Are you Mr Vasey?' Andrew asked.

The person, a man, was lit from behind, so Andrew couldn't see his face.

'Austin Vasey, yes.' The man flipped on a light above the door.

And another piece of the puzzle fell into place.

'It's you!' Andrew said. He was looking at a tall man with a small scar twisting the side of his mouth. 'You're the delivery driver!'

'I've no idea what you're talking about. Who are you?'

'You came to Tilda's shop with the mummy! It was you! I knew I was right.'

Vasey leaned out and looked at the car park. Andrew turned to look in the same direction – was something there?

'You'd better come in,' Vasey said, and stepped aside.

Andrew felt a bubble of excitement form in his chest. He'd been right! Vasey Construction had faked the curse. But why? It didn't make sense.

He found himself in a narrow corridor. Austin Vasey shut the door. And locked it.

The bubble leaked air. For a second, Andrew forgot to breathe. Vasey stood between him and the door. No one knew he was here. He wouldn't be missed for hours.

'In there.' Vasey pointed to a side door. Andrew turned

the handle, and was relieved to see that it was just an office – desk, chairs, computer, copier – all normal. He breathed again.

'Maybe you should tell me who you are and what you're doing here,' Vasey said.

'I'm Andrew. I was there when you brought the mummy, when you set the curse! Or, at least, I thought it was a curse. The vision and the smashed goblets and all that. But it was you all along, wasn't it?'

'I'm a businessman. I don't know anything about curses, or mummies. I've never seen you before in my life.'

Vasey moved around towards the desk and leaned against it. He looked calm, as though he didn't have a care in the world. Maybe Andrew was wrong? But no, he recognised him! It was definitely the same man!

'What I don't understand is why you did it,' Andrew said.

'Do your parents know you're out?'

'No. That isn't the point.'

'Does anyone?'

'No. Answer my question.'

'I don't know anything about curses, or fires, or anything you're talking about!'

Andrew paused.

A thick vein suddenly pumped in Vasey's neck.

'I didn't say anything about a fire,' Andrew said slowly.

Vasey had a sheen of sweat on his forehead. 'Didn't you? I must have misheard.'

'But there was a fire.'

Another piece of the puzzle clicked. This one so painful it almost knocked Andrew off his feet. He clutched the back of a chair and gripped hard until his knuckles were white.

'There were two fires,' Andrew whispered. 'At Tilda's and at the florist's Mum worked at. Last year. The firefighters never found out what happened. But it was you, wasn't it? You wanted the building, so you set a fire so you could get it cheaply. It happened early in the morning. Florists start early, you know. Maybe you didn't know. Maybe you didn't know she was inside when you set the fire? Do you know what happened to that florist's after the fire? It got demolished, then they built swanky flats on the site. Was it Vasey Construction who built them? It will be easy enough to find out. The police will be able to find out.'

Vasey snarled. 'So what if it was? That building was derelict.'

'Because you set fire to it.'

'That's a dangerous accusation to make.'

'My mum was in that fire!' The shout seemed to come from deep inside him. This man had hurt Mum! He was the reason she'd been so sick this past year. He was the reason she'd had to suffer. And all so he could sell some flats and make a profit.

'You don't know what you're talking about,' Vasey said. And tomorrow morning, I'll be meeting that idiot Benedict and his sappy aunt and she'll sign a deed of sale and hand over control to us. Before you know it there will be some lovely new flats on Marsh Road.'

'You're Benedict's investor?'

'That's what he thinks, but he'll be getting a nasty surprise once he reads the small print.'

'You won't get away with it!' Andrew yelled. He turned on his heel and rushed for the door. He was out of the office in seconds. He slammed against the front door and twisted the key in the lock. He took a sharp breath of clean air as he stumbled out.

But a hard knock from behind sent him clattering down the steps.

'Ow!' He landed heavily on the tarmac. He lay still, winded for a moment.

Then he felt arms tighten around his waist. He was lifted into the air. He saw the stars twinkling above, before a palm dropped over his eyes and everything was darkness.

Chapter Twenty-Six

Andrew's eyes blinked open. It made absolutely no difference. It was as dark with his eyelids open as it was with them closed. He could feel fabric against his eyelashes. He tried to lift his hands, to rub his eyes, but something pinned his hands together. He wriggled. Pins and needles shot through his legs, but he couldn't stretch out. Ropes. There were ropes at his wrists and ankles.

'Hello?' he called. His voice sounded weird, muffled, as though he were down a well.

Was he down a well? The thought was terrifying. But no, he didn't feel wet.

Where was he? What was he doing here?

His head ached, and it took a long time for him to marshal his thoughts into any kind of order. He'd been at the flat. Mum had woken in the night.

She'd been frightened. And then he'd gone to Vasey Construction.

Vasey.

Andrew remembered falling, and being bundled like some kind of parcel. He must have banged his head. Now he was more awake, it thumped in time to his heartbeat. The bruise was a whopper, he could tell already. He felt like an elephant had sat on his head.

He groaned. His wrists and ankles throbbed too, where the rope bit into them. He tried to sit up. He had to roll on to his side first. He felt groggy and wobbly, but he managed to sit upright.

Now what?

He felt tears prickle the back of his eyes.

No one knew where he was. Not even Andrew himself.

Mum would wake up in the flat with no idea what had happened to him. And while he was tied up here, Vasey would be at Meeke's, with Benedict, and Tilda would sign the shop over to them.

He pulled and tugged and wrenched at the ropes that held his hands behind his back, like a terrier worrying at a toy. All he did was sandpaper his wrists. But he couldn't stop. Mum and Tilda needed him to get free.

He twisted his arms and clawed, trying to grab the knot with his fingertips.

His little finger scratched against something sharp. He gasped with pain, but then he prodded the sharp thing carefully. It felt jagged and cold – a screw, or a nail, maybe? He rubbed the strands of rope against the head of the screw, sawing it back and forth. He ignored the ache in his limbs and the rough scraping against his skin. Back and forth, back and forth. Stopping every now and again to test the binding, seeing if it was fraying. Finally, he felt the strands of rope ping apart. With a hard tug he forced his hands outwards and the rope slithered to the ground. Blood tingled in his hands.

He yanked at the cloth over his eyes.

And blinked.

He was in a small space. Dark.

It was big enough for a chair, and some levers. He was sitting on the metal ground beside the chair.

He worked at the knots holding his feet together. It was hard to loosen them. His hands felt swollen and clumsy. But he did it eventually. The floor felt cold against his palms. He could see his breath float in white mist against the slate grey.

Andrew rolled on to his knees, then, gingerly, stood up, wincing as the blood rushed back into his feet.

Where was he?

The metal box had glass windows on all four sides, but the glass was murky with mud and grime. Beyond the glass was darkness. Were the windows fake? Was there nothing outside? Andrew spun around, searching for any clue to tell him where he was.

His eyes stopped on a glimmering paleness. It was partly hidden by the dirt on the glass, but he recognised it – the moon. So the box was outside and the blackness was the night sky.

He sighed. That was all right. All he had to do was get out of the box and he could go home.

He noticed a small handle set beside the seat. The outline of a door. He grabbed the handle and pressed. It didn't move. The door was locked. Well, that was to be expected. Vasey wouldn't tie him up then leave him in an unlocked room. That was OK. He'd smash the glass and get out that way.

And that was when he looked down.

A long way down.

And realised that the metal box he was trapped in was the control box of something much bigger. He was, he guessed, thirty metres off the ground in the tiny cabin of a crane. He could see the roof of Vasey Construction, and the other JCBs and diggers. He could feel a slight but definite sway as the cabin moved in the wind.

Smashing the glass didn't seem like such a good idea.

What on earth was he going to do now?

Chapter Twenty-Seven

Piotr woke to the sound of gentle tapping. 'Are you awake?' his mum whispered. 'There's a phone call for you.'

'Who is it?' Piotr pushed back his duvet and yawned. It was bound to be Andrew again, wanting to go off first thing to track down Vasey.

'It's Andrew's mum, Sarah.'

He frowned. That was weird. He headed out into the hall and took the phone from Mum. He saw his own worry reflected back in her face. Sarah never called, especially so early in the morning.

'Hello,' he said.

'Piotr, hi. Listen, is Andrew with you?'

He rubbed his eyes and balanced the phone under his chin while he let the implications of her question settle. 'No. He's not there?'

'No,' Andrew's mum said. 'His room is empty. Do you suppose he's at Minnie's? Or perhaps he just nipped to the shop?'

'That's probably it,' Piotr said, squishing his worry, trying his very best to keep his voice from shaking. 'He's probably just gone to get something nice for breakfast and forgot to leave a note. He'll be back any minute, I'm sure.'

'He's all right, isn't he? He's a sensible boy, really. Mostly. Sometimes.'

Piotr could hear the thin line of panic that laced her words. 'He's fine. I'm sure he's fine.'

What else could he say?

But he had a feeling that Andrew had done something stupid, and he wasn't fine at all.

As soon as he was off the phone to Mrs Jones, Piotr called Minnie. She hadn't seen or heard from Andrew since they'd left the cafe yesterday. 'I'll be at yours in fifteen minutes,' Piotr told her. Then he called Flora. Who hadn't seen Andrew either. She and Sylvie agreed to meet at the salon.

Piotr pulled on some clothes and grabbed an apple from the kitchen before saying goodbye to Mum – who looked more than a little worried herself, but let him leave without too much objection. He tried to eat it as he ran down the stairs and out of the flats, but it was difficult to swallow. He had a weird lump in his throat.

He got to the salon at the same time as the twins arrived from the opposite direction. Minnie let them all in.

'Andrew's really missing?' Flora said.

'It looks that way. His mum is trying not to worry, but he always leaves her a note when he goes out, and he didn't this time,' Piotr said.

'Where would he have gone?' Minnie asked. 'This doesn't make sense.'

'It does, I think.' Piotr dropped into the window seat. The smell of dyes and ammonias was making him feel light-headed.

'What do you mean?' Minnie snapped.

'He called me last night. He said he knew who had sent the mummy, who had faked the curse. He wanted to go and investigate, but I said it was too late, that we should wait for morning. I think he went without me. Without support. This is my fault.'

'It is not!' Sylvie said hotly. 'It's Andrew's own stupid fault and no one else's!'

'Sylvie!' Flora said sharply.

She blushed furiously. 'Sorry, sorry,' she said. 'I didn't mean that. I'm just so cross. What if he's in real trouble?'

Minnie and Flora shared a glance. An apology from Sylvie was as rare as unicorn's tears. Things were bad.

'What was his lead?' Flora asked.

Piotr explained quickly about the letter and Vasey Construction.

'Would he have gone there in the middle of the night?' Flora asked doubtfully.

Minnie shrugged. 'It's Andrew we're talking about.'

Flora took out her phone and tapped the screen. 'It's nearby,' she said. 'He might easily have gone there.' She walked towards the door. 'It's time to pay a visit to Vasey's. Who's coming with me?'

Andrew could see the cabin space clearly now that the sun was up. It was about the size of a kitchen table. The chair and dashboard took up most of the space. He'd settled into the chair when he realised that yelling wasn't doing any good at all. No one could hear him up here. There was a keyhole in the dash, to turn on the engine, but there was no sign of the key. The temperature in the confined space was rising. He could feel sweat itching in his hair. His throat felt dry and his tongue was weirdly swollen.

What time was it? He had no idea. Had Vasey made it to the shop? Had Tilda signed the deed of sale? Was it all too late?

He could barely move. He desperately wanted a drink. His stomach rumbled. And he couldn't stop thinking about Mum. Waking up and finding herself all alone. He wrapped his arms around his knees. Was he going to be trapped up here forever? What was Vasey going to do with him? Once he'd got Tilda to sign, would he let Andrew go? Or was he worried that Andrew knew too much? Was it too dangerous to let him out?

Would Mum think he'd run away?

That was the worst thing. Mum might think that he hadn't wanted to be with her any more. That he'd had enough of looking after her. She might think he'd abandoned her, just like Dad had done before he was born.

Andrew dashed the tears from his cheeks. He didn't have the water to spare.

'It's just along here somewhere,' Flora said, checking the address. The road was busy; cars inched bumper-to-tail with commuters heading to work; the sound of radio stations and the smell of coffee seeped from open windows. It all felt so ordinary.

But Piotr felt as though there was a shard of ice in his belly. Andrew was missing and, despite what he'd said to Sarah, he wasn't at all sure that Andrew was all right.

'Here,' Flora said.

The low, white building looked deserted. He checked his watch. Eight thirty. It was early, but he knew from his uncles and cousins that builders started work early. Was it odd that there was no one around? They walked warily past the squat brick wall and into the car park. Most of the spaces were empty – gravel filled the potholes in the concrete; the odd weed or dandelion poked up through the cracked ground. There were two cars; one had the dusty look of a car that hadn't been driven in a while. The other was a Fiat 500, an oversized bubblegum of a car. There was no sign of Andrew.

'Was he here?' Minnie asked.

'More importantly,' Flora replied, 'is he still here now?' She strode towards the steps that led to the front door. As she got within spitting distance, she stopped abruptly. Her hands flew to her ears. 'Ow!'

Piotr heard it too. And, judging by their pained faces, so did Minnie and Sylvie. A horrible, high-pitched whine that seemed to drill into his ears.

They all had their hands over their ears now.

'What is that?' Sylvie asked loudly.

'Mosquito!' Flora shouted. 'Like the one outside the newsagents to keep Lowdog away. But this one's much worse. It really hurts! Ow!' She stepped back, to get out of its range.

Just then, the door at the top of the steps opened. A woman in a crisp white vest and navy skirt stood in the entrance. She stared at the kids for a moment or two, then clapped her hand over her mouth. 'Sorry!' she said. Then clicked something on the wall beside her. The horrible noise stopped.

Piotr let his hands drop with a sigh of relief.

'Sorry, sorry!' the woman said. 'Mr Vasey must have set the Mosquito before he left last night. I didn't realise it was on. I can't hear it, you see. Though my nephew tells me it's nasty. I think Mr Vasey modified it a little. He likes to mess with gadgets. He might have gone too far with the Mosquito. But then, construction sites are dangerous places. It's probably best to discourage children.' The woman sounded doubtful.

'Is Mr Vasey here?' Piotr asked.

The woman shook her head. 'No, he has an urgent appointment this morning, closing a deal. He's not expected until this afternoon.'

'Have you seen a boy here? He's white, with dark hair and glasses?' Flora asked.

'A boy?' The woman tilted her head. 'What would a boy be doing here? There's no one here but me. I open up in the mornings. Have you been playing in the yard here? Those machines aren't toys, you know.'

Piotr didn't feel that the woman was hiding anything. She hadn't blushed or looked embarrassed when Flora asked about Andrew. He had the sense that she was simply there to work.

'His name is Andrew. If he doesn't turn up soon the police will be notified,' Flora said.

'How long has he been missing?' the woman said. 'Perhaps the police should be out looking. Poor wee mite. His parents must be worried.'

'Could we take a look around? See if he's hiding?' Minnie asked.

The woman tilted her head to one side sympathetically. 'I can't let you do that. But I promise I'll take a good look around right now. If he's climbed in an open window

183

and got stuck or something, I'll find him. But really, if he's missing, you should call the police. Good luck.'

With that she shut the door.

There was a horrible noise floating up to him from far below. Andrew struggled to climb out of the chair and look down. With his face pressed up to the grimy window, he could just about see into the car park.

A blue car that looked like a toy was parked there. It must have arrived when he was part dozing. It wasn't that making the nasty whine though. He caught a second of movement. There was someone there. Was Vasey back? Was he going to release him? Or was that not part of the plan?

Andrew wiped the glass with the edge of his hand. It became a touch clearer. It wasn't Vasey – it was Minnie! And Piotr! They were in the car park! And there were the twins! They'd come for him. Of course! He'd spoken to Piotr – he knew where to start looking. Andrew pounded the glass. 'Piotr! Up here! Minnie!' He pulled off a shoe and used that to smack the sides of the cabin. 'Help!' he yelled. 'Help!'

But no one down on the ground looked up.

* * *

184

'Did you hear something?' Piotr asked.

'Like what?' Flora said.

'I don't know, maybe it was nothing.' He looked behind him, out of the car park towards the road. The traffic had slowed to a standstill. Perhaps he'd just heard a horn beeping?

'We should call Jimmy,' Flora said firmly.

'Well, perhaps we should check with Andrew's mum first,' Minnie said. 'I mean, we don't know for sure that he came here. He might just have gone out early to buy milk or something and forgot to leave a note.'

'Do you really believe that?' Flora asked. 'I think we need Jimmy.'

Piotr knew in his heart that Flora was right. Andrew may or may not have been here. But there was no sign of him, and he could be anywhere by now. It was time to let the police know. Jimmy was an officer, but he was also their friend. It was time to walk away.

Chapter Twenty-Eight

Piotr's head drooped on his shoulders. The adrenalin that had surged through him when he heard that Andrew was missing had drained away, leaving him feeling torn and ragged. They hadn't found Andrew.

He scuffed the dirt with the tip of his trainer.

They were leaving with nothing.

And then, something on the ground glistened and sparkled, like a diamond catching the light.

He kicked it gently, freeing it from the tangle of straggly grass. It was a hair clip. A hair clip he recognised.

'Andrew was wearing this!' He bent down to pick it up. 'It was on his jeans pocket yesterday.'

He showed the clip to the others, cradling it in his palm as though it were a piece of treasure.

'So he was here!' Minnie said.

'I found it here, at the bottom of the steps.' Piotr

pointed. 'He might have left it here deliberately, as a clue for us. Or it might have dropped accidentally, if there was a struggle, or he fell.'

'A struggle?' Flora whispered the words.

Piotr imagined his friend, at night, alone, trying to pull free of someone's grasp, stumbling and falling on to the ground. His heart galloped in his chest. 'We have to find him. We have to find him now.'

Flora stood in the middle of the car park; she turned in a circle, looking in every direction. 'The woman isn't going to let us in the front door, but we can look through the windows, and we should check for a back door,' she said finally. 'And if we don't find him quickly, then we call Jimmy. Agreed?'

They all nodded solemnly. Finding the hair clip had changed everything. Andrew wasn't buying milk. He was in trouble.

There were a few windows on the front of the building. Piotr ducked below the first and rose slowly, fingertips pressed into the dirt on the edge of the sill. The room inched into view. Empty. No sign of a struggle. The next was the same. And the next. The others watched anxiously. He shook his head. No sign of Andrew.

They crept around the side of the building towards the yard. Maybe there was a back door they could try?

High above their heads, Andrew watched his four friends creep closer. But they weren't looking up. He took off his other shoe, and, wearing them on his palms, he pounded the side of the cabin. Hard. Again and again and again.

'Can you hear that?' Piotr asked as they stepped into the yard. There was a faint banging noise. Too urgent to be hammering. The wrong sound for a car alarm.

He scanned the area. On his right was the office block, white walls, a blue emergency exit and concrete ramp, a gutter flecked with last autumn's leaves. In front of him, three JCBs, yellow, speckled with brown patches of rust, their huge caterpillar tracks clogged with old mud and clay. A small crane. A cherry picker. All grimy from months or years spent outside. No signs of life at all.

Where was the noise coming from?

Minnie, beside him, shaded her eyes and looked too. Left, right. Then up.

She gasped.

'There's something up there!' She pointed to the top of the crane. 'Something at the window!'

Piotr screwed up his eyes. He could just about make out the movement that Minnie meant. And the sound seemed to be centred on the cabin.

'Why is the cabin up there?' Flora asked. 'When it was used last, the controller would have got out on the ground. Not all the way up there.'

'Unless the person who was in it last hasn't come down yet,' Sylvie said grimly.

'Andrew!' Piotr yelled. 'Andrew!'

The banging reached a crescendo, as though the person making the noise was trying to reply.

'Andrew! We need to get him down.'

Piotr raced over to the crane. Its base was solid, square, with tracks, like a miniature rail line pointing up to the sky. The cabin was at the top of the tracks. It might be possible to climb up the tracks. But how could they get Andrew out of the cabin? 'We need a key,' he said.

Minnie looked back at the office building. 'I'm on it,' she said.

She raced around to the front of the building and pounded on the door.

It opened in moments and the woman frowned down. 'You again?'

'We've found our friend. He's trapped in the cabin of the crane.'

The woman's eyebrows shot up. 'He's in the crane? That's crazy! He could get hurt. Tell him to get out, right now.'

'If he gets out right now, he'll fall thirty metres to the ground.'

'The cabin's in the air?' The woman's voice soared a pitch higher.

'Do you have the key?' Minnie asked.

The woman swayed a little, unsure whether to rush into the building, or to rush out. 'The keys are kept in the desk drawer.'

'Can you get the key for the crane? Can you get the cabin down?'

'Operate the crane?' The woman's face paled. 'I don't know how. I'm not qualified.'

'Well, get me the key and I'll do it,' Minnie said.

'You're definitely not qualified! OK, wait there. I'll do my best.'

She stepped back inside. The door stayed ajar and Minnie could see her rush into a side office; then she heard her rifling through a drawer. The clink of metal. A drawer slammed shut.

Then the woman was back. She held up a key on a thick leather fob. 'This is it.' Her voice shook.

'Don't worry,' Minnie said. 'I'm sure driving a crane isn't that different to driving a Fiat 500. Come on.' She took the woman's arm and pulled her around the building to the yard.

'What's your name?' Minnie asked.

'Samantha. Sam.'

'Well, Sam, you're going to be fine. You're going to rescue our friend and be a hero. OK?'

'OK. Yes. OK.'

The others stepped back to allow Sam to reach the crane. She slipped a key into a metal box on the side of the base. A little door swung open. Inside was a chunky keyhole, and some plastic-covered buttons. Two green. One red.

Sam took a deep breath. She pushed a bigger key into the hole and turned it. There was a low growl as the engine whirred into life.

'You're doing great!' Minnie said, eyeing the cabin anxiously.

'I think it's this one. Or this one,' Sam said. Her fingers hovered over the two green buttons. 'It's not this one. Probably.' She tapped the red one. The crane juddered.

'Careful!' Flora warned.

'Sorry. It's this one.' She pressed one of the green buttons firmly.

And the cabin began a gentle descent down towards the ground.

Chapter Twenty-Nine

Andrew could have cried with relief as the cabin began to move. The ground got closer and closer. He pressed his palms against the glass. *Get the door open, get the door open*, he thought, over and over.

Minnie was the first to reach up and try the door handle. She found it was locked. He could see her gesturing to someone. Then there were keys in her hand. A scrape in the lock. And the door swung open.

Andrew took great lungfuls of freezing-cold air.

He was free.

The others reached to help him down, he was lifted by them, just for a moment, floating in mid-air, held up by their strength. Then his feet were on solid ground again. In socks. Piotr climbed up to fetch his shoes.

'What time is it?' Andrew asked, his throat hoarse from shouting.

Flora checked her watch. 'Nearly nine. Wait. Are you OK? Are you hurt? Who did this to you?'

'Austin Vasey,' Andrew said.

A woman, who he noticed for the first time, gasped. 'Mr Vasey? Why? Why would he do that?'

'To shut me up,' Andrew said. 'But no one can shut me up – I've got school reports to prove it!' He steadied himself against Piotr as he pulled on his shoes. 'Right. We have to get to Meeke's before Vasey does. But first, I need to speak to Mum. Can I borrow someone's phone?'

Flora's phone was in his hand instantly. Already ringing his number. Mum answered on the first ring.

'Andrew?' she asked. The worry in her voice was like a shard of steel in his heart.

'It's me. I'm all right. I'm sorry.'

'Where have you been? What's going on?'

'I can't explain now. I have to get to Meeke's. But I will explain properly, very soon. I just wanted you to know I was safe. I love you.'

'Andrew! Andrew!'

He finished the call and handed the phone back to Flora. 'Come on,' he said, 'I'm not the only one who needs saving today.'

* * *

Minnie was in front the whole way as they raced across town, darting between stomping commuters, using lamp posts as pivots to spin her way through sharp turns. Piotr was next, head down, running like he was on the sports track. Andrew and Flora weren't far behind, gasping and panting, but keeping up. Sylvie trailed at the back, wailing something about her shoes being too tight for long distance.

'Andrew, what … oof … what has Vasey got to do … oof … with the curse?' Flora asked as they ran.

Andrew, gripping a stitch in his side, could barely breathe, let alone answer. 'Tell you when we get there,' he managed.

They'd reached Marsh Road. The colour, sound, smells of the market rushed past. A few people yelled after them as they ran through, telling them to slow down, but the cries were already lost. Andrew leaped a cardboard box and landed upright. He felt like a superhero!

Minnie and Piotr were waiting, panting, outside Meeke's. Inside, Andrew could see Tilda, and Benedict – and Austin Vasey.

'Ready?' Piotr asked.

Andrew wiped the sweat from his forehead with the back of his sleeve. 'Ready,' he said.

Chapter Thirty

Andrew burst into Meeke and Sons Curios and Gimcracks just as Tilda's pen hovered over a sheet of paper.

'Stop!' Andrew yelled.

Tilda's hand froze.

'What's going on? What's the meaning of this?' Benedict asked. He frowned, definitely annoyed.

But Austin Vasey looked scared. His dark eyebrows had shot up at the sight of Andrew. His lips were pressed together tightly so that his scar looked like a pale worm on his lip. 'Ms Meeke,' he said, 'your signature, if you would be so kind.'

'Don't sign that paper!' Andrew insisted.

They were all inside the shop now, clustered in the doorway. Tilda and the other grown-ups were standing around the refectory table, as though they were at a meeting.

Andrew strode in, taking his place at the head of the table.

'Austin Vasey is a crook and a thief. And he hurt my mum!'

Benedict took a step away from Vasey.

'He was the one who stole the mummy from Miranda. He sent it here with a forged letter that made us believe there was a curse, and then he made Tilda think she was seeing visions, and that the shop was haunted, and then, when he was getting desperate, he started a fire, just like he did with the florist's last year!'

Austin Vasey pulled himself up to his full height. 'This child is a fantasist! A liar! I have no idea what he's talking about.'

Benedict gripped the edge of the table. 'Is it true? Did you start the fire?'

'Of course not,' Vasey snapped. 'Why would I do such a thing?'

'To force Tilda into handing over the shop to you and Benedict!' Andrew said. 'What are you going to do? Turn it into more flats?'

Benedict shook his head. 'Mr Vasey is coming in as a silent partner in the business. A few weeks ago he approached me and offered to fund the refurbishment of the shop. We'll knock through to the back, make the display area bigger and brighter, and make the whole place look more modern. But flats? Never! This has been Meeke's for generations. I would never change that.'

Andrew saw Minnie and the others move up alongside him. His friends were with him. 'Austin Vasey has been lying to you. As soon as Tilda was out of the picture, he'd take the business from you. There's bound to be something in the small print of that contract. He's tricked you too, just like he tricked Tilda with the curse.'

Flora gasped. 'The vision! I know how he did it!'

Tilda threw her pen down on to the table. 'I'm not signing this until I've heard everything these children have to say, and that's that.'

Austin Vasey edged around the table. 'Well, if now isn't a good time, I can come back later.'

Benedict blocked his path. 'You, sit. I want to hear what these children have to say too. I trusted you. I thought you had the best interests of the shop at heart. If I find you did anything to hurt my family, I promise, you will regret it. Sit!' He barked the command and Vasey dropped into an ornately carved wooden chair.

Flora moved towards the window, and looked up. 'This shop is directly opposite the construction site. Anyone standing up on the scaffolding would have a direct view of the front of the shop. Tilda, do you remember you told us that you saw a sudden flash? Just before the vision appeared? I bet that someone on that building site had just taken the lens cap off a projector. It caught the sunlight and you saw the light reflected in the lens. And then they projected the image of the Eye of Ra on to the wall, just for a second, just for long enough to frighten you.'

Tilda's hands flew to cover her mouth, which had fallen open in dismay.

'We know Mr Vasey likes to use technology,' Minnie said. 'Samantha at his office says he's always meddling with gadgets.'

'Like the Mosquito,' Piotr added.

'Horrible thing,' Sylvie said. 'That nasty noise made me want to smash it, and I'm not a violent person.'

Flora grinned at that.

Then, her mouth fell open too. 'Sylvie, you're a genius!' she said. 'That's how he broke the goblets! If you play a certain frequency intensely enough, glass will vibrate and shatter of its own accord! That's why building glass bridges is a terrible idea!'

'Glass bridges?' Andrew asked.

'Take my word for it,' Flora replied.

Minnie rushed over to the cabinet and crouched to look at the lower shelves, then stretched to look at the top. 'There was a vase here. On Monday, there was a vase. I saw Vasey pick it up when he was disguised as a delivery driver. He must have dropped the Mosquito inside it then.'

'I sold it,' Tilda said. 'A man came in on Wednesday morning, after we'd cleared up the broken glass, and bought it. He said it was for his mum.'

'Was it an accomplice?' Piotr asked Vasey. 'Or was it you in disguise?'

'This is all hearsay and speculation!' Vasey shouted. 'There is not one speck or trace of actual evidence that I have done anything other than offer to help Benedict spruce up an untidy shop. And last time I checked, redecorating isn't a crime.'

Just at that moment, the bell above the door jangled.

'Andrew!' Mum ran into the shop. Followed by Jimmy in his police uniform.

Andrew felt his heart leap. Mum was out of the house! Back in the shop. And, despite the fact that she looked furious, he was so pleased to see her.

She smothered him in an angry hug. 'Where have you been? I've been worried sick. I called Jimmy.'

'Sorry,' he said into the soft wool of her cardigan. 'I got a bit carried away.'

He hugged her back as tightly as he could.

Then felt her stiffen. It was as though a switch had been thrown in her body.

'Who's he?' she whispered.

He stepped out of her arms and followed her gaze. She was staring at Austin Vasey.

'He's a very bad man,' Sylvie said.

'I know his face. He's been in my dreams.' Mum sounded confused, frightened. 'How do I know his face?'

'He delivered the parcel here on Monday,' Piotr suggested.

Mum shook her head. 'He was there! At the shop last year, before the fire! I saw him pass by the window. I remember now.'

Andrew slipped his hand under her elbow. She was shaking, her face pale. 'Why was he there?'

'Jimmy,' Flora said, 'we suspect that this man, Austin Vasey, has been starting fires in shops, and buying them cheaply. He's been trying to frighten Tilda into giving him this shop.'

Jimmy took out his notebook. 'There was a scene of crime officer sent here last night to investigate the fire. I think they would be very interested in looking again at the evidence collected from the florist's last year to see if there's a connection. With your mum able to place Mr Vasey at the scene they will be very interested indeed.'

'And don't forget he locked me at the top of a crane!' Andrew said cheerfully.

'What?' Mum shrieked.

'Don't worry, his nice assistant got me down again.'

'Mr Vasey,' Jimmy said, in his most stern voice, 'I suggest you come with me down to the station.'

Chapter Thirty-One

On Monday morning, Andrew helped Mum into an imaginary rocket.

They blasted off together out from the flats, past the bench and on to Marsh Road. Mum was the lead pilot; Andrew was just there to watch out for passing asteroids and space junk.

'Abandoned shopping trolley on port side!' Andrew yelled.

'Taking evasive action,' Mum replied.

She'd had three good nights' sleep. It had made all the difference. Knowing that the person responsible for her injuries was locked up, awaiting trial, had helped too.

'I'll pick up some provisions on my way home from the space station tonight,' Mum said. 'I'm thinking stuffed peppers with spicy rice?'

'Not beans?' Andrew asked hopefully.

'I think we can do a bit better than that, don't you?' Mum steered the rocket down the perilous debris belt that was Marsh Road and executed a perfect landing outside Meeke and Sons.

'Do you want me to come inside?' Andrew asked.

Mum shook her head. 'Absolutely not. Tilda and I have got lots of work to get on with if I'm going to learn how to run the shop while she's away.'

Tilda and Benedict were planning a fortnight by the sea, so that they could both recover. Mum and Miranda would mind the shop while they were gone. With Bruiser standing guard against badly behaved cats.

'Look,' Mum said. 'You should go and join them.'

Andrew looked.

Piotr and Minnie and Flora and Sylvie were sitting in the window seat of the cafe. Piotr gave him a wave.

Mum didn't need him any more.

He wasn't sure how he felt. For about three seconds. Then he whooped with delight. 'I bet we find another mystery to solve by lunchtime!' he said.

Mum laughed. 'Why don't you just have a milkshake and see what the day brings?'

Andrew gave Mum a quick hug. And let her walk on alone.

He headed towards the cafe. Where his friends were waiting.

Read on for some
top-secret character stats
on the Marsh Road
investigators!

THE MARSH ROAD MYSTERIES

FLORA HAMPSHIRE

Good things come in small packages, and there are few people as good as the youngest twin (by five minutes) Flora. She's always ready with a kind word, or a helping hand, or a disgusting fact if that's what the situation calls for. Her book of forensic science is never far from reach. And her note-taking is the very best in the business.

Brain power:	10
Friendship factor:	9
Honesty:	9
Bravery:	6
Sleuthing:	9
Self-confidence:	4

SYLVIE HAMPSHIRE

The older of the two twins (by five minutes), Diva is Sylvie Hampshire's middle name. As a promising young actress, she demands the limelight. She'd rather be making waves than making friends. As long as her blood sugar is fine, there's nothing that can stop her getting to the top. It's been that way ever since Mum and Dad split up.

Brain power:	7
Friendship factor:	3
Honesty:	4
Bravery:	9
Sleuthing:	6
Self-confidence:	10

THE MARSH ROAD MYSTERIES

PIOTR DOMEK

Somehow, to his surprise, Piotr leads the gang of investigators. He isn't sure quite how that happened – the job just landed on him. Luckily, he wasn't hurt. Now he has to put down his comic books and pick up the reins. Who knows where he might end up?

Brain power: **8**

Friendship factor: **9**

Honesty: **10**

Bravery: **9**

Sleuthing: **8**

Self-confidence: **5**

THE MARSH ROAD MYSTERIES

MINNIE ADESINA

Minnie is as tall and as prickly as the branches of a holly tree, but her heart is firmly in the right place. Once she's your friend, she's your friend forever. On rainy days, when there's no mystery to be solved, Minnie can be found treating Mum's nail polishes like magic potions. It almost counts as a hobby.

Brain power:	7
Friendship factor:	10
Honesty:	6
Bravery:	9
Sleuthing:	7
Self-confidence:	8

THE MARSH ROAD MYSTERIES

ANDREW JONES

The whole world is a stage, as far as Andrew is concerned, and he is the leading man. And every other role too, if he can get his hands on the script. He loves to be the centre of attention and is always ready to take a risk. In his less dramatic moments, he helps take care of his mum.

Brain power: **7**

Friendship factor: **8**

Honesty: **5**

Bravery: **10**

Sleuthing: **8**

Self-confidence: **9**

Look out for the next instalment of

The MARSH ROAD MYSTERIES

Dogs and Doctors

Coming 2017